She made to walk past him, but a hand shot out and he pulled her back. She could feel his fingers like a vice through her coat sleeve. 'Let me go!' she managed to say, prising uselessly at his fingers.

'I still might have this whole incident opened up. Your answers are by no means satisfactory,' he replied grimly, all vestige of humour gone now, so that her first sneaking suspicion that he was merely giving her a hard time for the perverse pleasure it gave him was swept aside.

She flung back her head, platinum-blonde spikes brushing his chin, and he flinched back as if he expected her to hit him with her free hand, but his grip tightened and she stamped her foot in frustration.

'Wild little thing, aren't you?' he murmured close to her ear. 'Now, tell me who sent you.'

HAZARD
OF LOVE

BY

SALLY HEYWOOD

MILLS & BOON LIMITED
ETON HOUSE 18-24 PARADISE ROAD
RICHMOND SURREY TW9 1SR

First published in Great Britain 1989
by Mills & Boon Limited

© Sally Heywood 1989

Australian copyright 1989
Philippine copyright 1990
This edition 1990

ISBN 0 263 76518 0

Set in English Times 12 on 12½ pt.
01 – 9001 – 38050

Typeset in Great Britain by JCL Graphics, Bristol

Made and Printed in Great Britain

CHAPTER ONE

GOLDIE knew she was wearing the wrong clothes the minute she stepped inside the front door. A sea of country tweeds and waxed jackets flowed slowly ahead of her along the passage towards the open doors of the sitting-room. She should have remembered. This was Yorkshire, not California; farming country, not a Hollywood film set.

She glanced down at her high-heeled ankle boots with the silver heels, and then at the sensible brogues and lace-ups of the people queueing to go in ahead of her. The glance took in her long, slender legs, the deep tan almost visible beneath the sheer nylons she had had to buy at the airport, having forgotten such things existed in the hurry of departure.

She cringed inside and tried to pull her tiny mini down to a more discreet level, failing miserably. Already odd looks were being cast in her direction. Though tiny and childishly slender, she was eye-catching anyway, but here with her golden tan and short, spiky platinum-blonde hair, and what now seemed outlandish get-up, she felt as if she stuck out like a sore thumb. And she had hoped that her return would pass unnoticed!

A middle-aged matron in a tweed skirt and jacket was adding to the stares, eyes puzzled as she tried to name the face. Goldie dropped her glance. She couldn't get out now without causing even more of an upheaval, because people were already crowding round the front porch to get in out of the rain. Help, she thought, I should have thought this through before charging off without a proper plan!

The woman said something to her companion, an elderly man in a Barbour, Langdale cap and glasses, and he, too, turned to stare at her. His glance flicked over her face without recognition, then suddenly the woman said something and they both began to smile. 'It's Goldie, isn't it?' she called between the intervening heads. People in front of Goldie turned round, too, then faced front smartly as she swept them with a cool stare in return. The woman was now beginning to push her way back along the queue. 'I'd recognise you anywhere, my dear. You're the spitting image of your mother. How is she?'

'Very well, thank you.' Goldie felt mystified, and not a little embarrassed. Ought she to be able to remember who this person was?

As if reading her thoughts, the woman said,

'You won't remember me. We live next door to your aunt.' She gestured in the general direction of the garden, and then looked contrite. 'I mean, lived next door—oh, dear, so tragic and so sudden.' Her expression changed. 'I didn't see you or Ravella at the funeral.' Although it was a statement, the question was implicit.

Goldie felt distinctly uncomfortable, knowing exactly what was going through the woman's mind. 'We were all away on location at the time. I only got back two days ago, and the solicitor's letter telling me of Aunt Eva's death was waiting for me then. Mother's still filming in the Far East, and doesn't know about it even now. She'll be heartbroken,' she added defensively.

'Of course she will.' The woman accepted her explanation at once, adding warmly, 'Ravella was very happy in the time she was here. And she and Eva were so very fond of each other.'

This was no surprise to Goldie, but it made her feel a little glow inside to hear it said. There was something genuine about the woman, and she realised she'd become too used to the flip heartlessness of the people she worked with. The lack of any real depth of feeling in her everyday relationships had made her forget what natural warmth was like.

By this time the woman's husband had joined them. 'By jove!' he exclaimed as he reached for Goldie's hand. 'You were a little whipper-snapper of twelve or so last time I saw you. I'm Sam Woollard.' He shook her briskly by the hand and turned to his wife. 'Hetty, are we taking this young lady back home for afternoon tea after this scrum's over?'

'I really don't think——' began Goldie, then checked herself. She had nowhere to go afterwards. Her most pressing problem was to find a hotel for the night, then plan what to do next. She had whipped out of her apartment without giving the matter any thought at all, and on the flight over had slept most of the time, too tired by the previous six weeks' filming to do anything else.

Mrs Woollard eyed her kindly. 'If you've time, we'd be delighted, Goldie. We're all so proud of you both, you know. We don't have many celebrities in Little Skidby.' She patted Goldie on the arm. 'I think we'd better go in to the sale now. It's due to start in a few minutes.'

Goldie nodded and followed, childhood memories surging back the minute she set foot in the high-ceilinged drawing-room. How changed everything was, with rows of chairs set out in preparation for the auction of Eva's furniture and effects. Tables and cupboards, footstools and bedheads, all sickeningly familiar, were stacked along the walls with little familiar objects, vases and boxes and other trinkets she had long forgotten, grouped on every surface.

'So tragic that this should all go to strangers,' Mrs Woollard said as they took their seats somewhere in the middle. 'Eva thought she was immortal. Indeed, I think we all did, didn't we, Sam?' She gave Goldie a sympathetic glance. 'I heard that in her will she asked for the proceeds of this sale to be divided between Ravella and Eva's favourite charity, but the furniture is so lovely, I'm sure you or Ravella would have welcomed it.'

Looking round, Goldie wasn't so sure about her mother welcoming a lot of old English furniture in the luxurious ultra-modern penthouse in Bel Air which she shared with her latest live-in lover. There was nothing traditional about her mother, either in life-style or taste. She sighed.

'I'm not very settled,' she admitted to Mrs Woollard. 'I would have loved some of Eva's things for old times' sake, and I wouldn't have minded buying some of it back, if only I had somewhere to put it. But it would be hopeless

trying to take any of this back to California.'
Her eye travelled slowly over the lovely but
large and cumbersome pieces. 'I'm just here to
say goodbye to everything, really,' she
confessed.

'You're not settled with a husband, then?'

Goldie shook her head, not offended by the
question, knowing that such bluntness was the
way in these parts. 'I can't see me married!'
She made a joke of it, but felt a twinge of
sadness at the thought. It wasn't that she had
anything against marriage as such, it was just
the example of other people's marriages that
put her off. They were almost always followed
by divorce and acrimony. And she didn't want
that.

Nor did she intend to live with someone as
her mother did, changing lovers when they
became boring, as one might change a coat
that had gone out of fashion.

She wanted something else, but she didn't
know what, and she couldn't escape the feeling
that maybe she was just an old-fashioned
idealist—if she wasn't careful she would finish
up unmarried and childless like Eva, with all
the things that added up to her life going to
strangers when she died.

'Here, have a look at the catalogue.' Sam
pushed several sheets of printed foolscap into
her hand. She hadn't thought of catalogues.

Now she skimmed it rapidly as the auctioneer took his place at the front and made a few announcements.

She was searching out the one thing she hoped was here, for if she could take anything back, then that was it. Her eyes alighted on lot sixty-three. A painting in oils, it said, rendered in the Impressionist manner by local artist Brendan Halliwell. Subject, Mother and Child. She knew the painting intimately. It had hung in Eva's sitting-room over the roll-top desk for as long as she could remember. But where was it now?

Her glance roamed the room again as the bidding started, then she gave a smile of satisfaction. A large wardrobe had been trundled out of place and there, behind it, propped on top of an oak and gilt console-table, was the painting.

Framed now in a pale border of carved beech, its soft pinks and blues and mauves seemed to sing softly of a time long ago in a distant land when everything had been safe and unchanging. A woman, long fair hair trailing over one shoulder in soft tendrils, and wearing an expression of rapt concern on the beautiful oval of her face, was holding a small baby among the folds of a long blue gown. That there were references to a million portraits of Madonna and Child, Goldie could

see now, but when, as a child herself, she had
stood wrapped in the warmth and tranquillity
of the picture, she had known none of this. To
her it was simply her mother holding her on
her lap, for she had been three when she had
realised that the woman in the picture was her
own mother, and the baby, the baby in her
arms, was herself, being held with all the
loving care she had yearned for.

Somehow, just being able to come and look
at 'Aunty Eva's picture' had seemed to make
up for the neglect she had been so sorely
conscious of in those days. Just beginning to
make her way in films, her mother had been
away so often and sometimes for so long,
and no one seemed to appreciate how much
the tiny child missed her. It had helped
to be able to come and look at the picture, for
it seemed to prove that she had once been
loved, had once had all her mother's loving
care.

She came to with a start. Bidding had
started and lots were being rapidly wheeled on
and off. Soon she would have to catch the
auctioneer's eye. She bit her lip. She had never
done this sort of thing before. She turned to
Mrs Woollard, hoping for some advice, but
she was gazing intently at the auctioneer.
Goldie saw her give a little nod. Then the
hammer fell and she turned to Goldie with a

smile. 'Oh, I am pleased. That's Eva's sweet little sewing-basket. Always in a jumble, it was—I was forever tidying it up for her.' She wiped the corner of an eye. Goldie put out a hand and patted her on the arm. It was like coming home. She hadn't expected to feel like this.

'I'd like the picture,' she confessed in a whisper. 'It's of Mother and me.'

Mrs Woollard nodded. 'Very nice it is, too.'

Soon the painting was being held up by one of the assistants as the auctioneer gave a brief description. 'Shall we start at, say, one hundred pounds? One hundred am I bid?' There was a murmur of interest. Goldie smiled to herself. She could afford to spend whatever it took. Why not? It was a little piece of her past. It had been her comfort long years ago. She owed it to herself to buy it so that she could give it a home where its true worth could be appreciated.

She managed to catch the auctioneer's eye, and when he said, 'Am I bid one-twenty? One-thirty?' she kept on nodding. Three or four would-be purchasers dropped out, and soon she became aware that there were only two of them left. With frightening speed the bidding seemed to have shot up to five hundred, then five-twenty. A hush had fallen over the room and she found she was holding her breath. It was like being on a roller-coaster, but she couldn't get off. The auctioneer was glancing from one side of the room to the other. First to herself, then to the other bidder.

Daring to turn her head for a moment, she could just see the back of a man's head at the end of the row in front. She saw him nod again and, anticipating the auctioneer's eye, she nodded, too. Six hundred pounds? When on earth was the other chap going to stop? She was swept along. Soon it reached a thousand. A pin dropping would have shattered the silence.

Goldie felt herself grow hot. Why was he bidding so fiercely? It was ridiculous. Surely the painting was only special to the people in it? As far as she knew, Brendan Halliwell had never been particularly famous.

The auctioneer must have thought the same, for he now wore an expression of interested surprise. His eyebrows rose first left, then right. It was like the final game in a tennis match. The tension was unbearable. 'Drop out, damn you,' Goldie found herself muttering beneath her breath. Then there was a sudden break in the rising tide of bids. The auctioneer held up his gavel, and for one wild moment Goldie imagined he was going to knock it down to her, but instead he was leaning forward over his desk. 'Yes, sir? An objection?'

To Goldie's amazement she heard a voice from the row in front ask if it was certain the bidder was able to hand over the sum lot sixty-three had already reached. 'Bearing in mind,' came the clipped English accent, 'that this particular auction house usually requires a written bank guarantee for sums over one thousand pounds.'

Suddenly she found everyone on either side stiffening in their seats as they restrained themselves from turning to stare.

'Yes, ma'am? Did you hear the objection?' The auctioneer smiled encouragingly.

She nodded, confused. How much cash had she converted into sterling at the airport? Not much. She didn't believe in carrying too much in case she was mugged. But she had a card. That was usually all she needed. Her blood froze. What an idiot she was! Of course she couldn't pay by card. It had to be cheque with a guarantee or cash. Not knowing what to do, she simply gazed straight ahead, trying not to feel conscious of the interest she was arousing. She felt all wrong again, in her big coat with its huge padded shoulders—a coat that had seemed so fashionable, so right in the city, and was a concession to English weather, but now, in the depths of the Yorkshire countryside, looked too flamboyant, too theatrical and therefore, in the eyes of the people here, too unreliable by half.

The tweed shoulders and short dark hair of her rival on the next row mocked her for her flightiness, and she slowly unclenched her tightly balled fists. What on earth could she do?

'The penalty this auction house levies for bidding with insufficient resources, if I may just remind everyone,' the auctioneer looked round at the roomful of people, tactfully taking the pressure off Goldie for a moment, 'is ten per cent of the bid price, plus VAT, plus administration charges for representing the lot at a later date.' He beamed. 'Where were we? Two thousand four hundred and sixty pounds, I believe. Madam? Mr de Maine?'

He knows his name, registered Goldie furiously. He would have no problems producing a bank guarantee out of a hat! This oh, so financially sound Mr de Maine. She remembered the name herself from all those years ago. They owned practically everything. Old Mr de Maine and his rolling hills stretching up to the moors. Her rival for the picture must be one of his clan. Her hackles rose.

The auctioneer raised his hammer. Goldie gave another little nod.

'Two thousand four hundred and seventy—and eighty?'

Surely I can get the money? thought Goldie frantically. She could do it almost straight away. All she had to do was go to the nearest American Express office. She could walk away with thousands bundled up in her bag. If there was an American Express office in this backwater. If it wasn't Saturday afternoon. And if only the bidding could be halted while she called a cab . . . Miserably she gazed straight ahead. She'd lost. There was no point in pretending. She dared not go on any longer. It would simply be too embarrassing if they refused to take a cheque without a guarantee. In a daze of disappointment, she heard the auctioneer raise the bid another twenty and she saw the hammer come down.

'To Mr de Maine at two thousand five hundred pounds. Thank you, sir.' The auctioneer looked pleased and mopped his brow with a large red handkerchief.

Goldie, wedged in the middle of a row, sat out the rest of the sale in a state of misery.

Sam and Hetty gave her sympathetic glances. 'Never mind, lass. You certainly made him pay through the nose for it.'

She couldn't tell what they thought about that, for their expressions were non-committal. It was clear what other people thought, though. Looking at her, they imagined she was some silly young girl who'd made a public fool of herself. It was worse later. As she was making her way towards the door, stuck fast in the throng of people all with the same idea, she overheard someone say, 'There she is. Bidded him up nice and proper, I reckon. If it was me, I'd ask for an inquiry.'

Another voice chimed in, 'They should make the rules clear at the beginning. She probably didn't realise.'

'He'd probably have got it for a couple of hundred if she hadn't pushed the price up.'

She found a gap in the crowd and slid through it, coming out in the corridor leading, as she remembered, to the kitchen. Her only wish now was to escape from all these people who had seemed to represent a lost childhood, but now represented only humiliation and regret.

Thankfully, she slipped inside and closed the door, leaning against it and trying to steady her breathing. But her respite was short-lived. Voices out in the passage sent her moving into the middle of the room, turning defensively as the door opened. A tall, broad-shouldered farming type came in, calling back over his shoulder, 'Don't let her get up, I'll bring it out to her.' He skidded to a sudden halt when he caught sight of Goldie. She was conscious of bark-brown eyes in a youngish face looking her over from top to toe, and then a sudden derisive tightening of lips that were really too full for good looks.

'Oh, it's you,' he said, with no attempt at politeness. He pushed past her to reach the sink and she watched him turn on the cold water, drawing off enough to fill a glass. 'Someone's feeling faint out there. Probably at the thought of sitting next to a two-and-a-half-thousand-pound painting.' The glass filled, he made for the door again, turning briefly when he reached it, saying, 'Don't go, I want a word with you.'

Goldie watched him disappear in amazement. It was only when she caught a glimpse of the back of his tweed shoulders, with that head of short, dark glossy hair, that memory stirred. Of course, it had to be—the man in the saleroom. The one she had forced to bid up for a painting that was probably only worth a few hundred. She felt blood swarm into her cheeks and her first thought was escape, but before she could move he was back, and, closing the door behind him, he began to advance slowly towards her.

'That's that sorted out. Now to sort you out.' He was almost on top of her when he came to a halt, and she was shiveringly aware of how big and broad-shouldered he was in his thorn-proof tweeds and husky Aran sweater, but before she could sort out her feelings he snarled, 'So why the hell did you do that?' His voice, though fierce, was quiet—as if to conceal the fact that he was about to launch a verbal attack. 'Do you realise,' he went on, 'I could have the whole thing assessed and land you with a hell of a bill? Apart from any other more personal revenge I might want to take. What then?'

Almost despite himself, his glance scudded over her body again, taking in the skimpy T-shirt and too-short mini with the little boots that had seemed cute when she had bought them, but now seemed suddenly bizarre. She began to draw the oversized coat around herself. It kept slipping off her shoulders. In the city it looked merely stylish like that—here it seemed deliberately provocative. The effect was not lost on her adversary, and seeing it she lifted her chin and tried to give him her coldest stare.

'I take it you're Mr de Maine?'

'Who the hell else? Look, just answer me, who sent you? Ravella Eastwood?'

She felt bewildered. 'I don't know what you mean. Why should anyone send me? I'm quite capable of deciding where and when I travel——'

'Don't play games with me, sweetheart,' he broke in. 'You've just cost me one and a half thousand over the odds. There has to be a reason.'

She recognised that he had a right to be angry, but she felt too scared to be seen to agree, in case he really did carry out his threat to get the whole thing assessed. She didn't know what that meant, but it sounded stuffy and legal and very humiliating.

'I don't understand English customs,' she explained. 'I honestly thought I'd have enough cash on me to pay for it. Then when it shot up like that I suppose I imagined I could pay by credit card or something.' She shrugged. 'I didn't know there was all this stuff about bank guarantees. Back home my name's enough to guarantee anything I want to buy.'

'Back home? The States?'

'I'm surprised you've heard of it,' she said before she could stop herself, provoked beyond reason by his cutting tones.

His expression hardened. 'So we're all country hicks out here, are we?' His lips curved back in a mirthless smile. 'I've got news for you. Some of us have actually walked to the end of the lane and back.' He suddenly peered closer. 'The coincidence is too much. Ravella was in California last time I heard. And you freely admit your home is the States——'

'Add it up and you might get ninety-two!' she retorted, angry now that her fear had abated somewhat. 'It's not my fault I don't know your stupid rules. Nor do I see why I should stand here and be cross-questioned by you, Mr de Maine.'

She made to walk past him, but a hand shot out and he pulled her back. She could feel his fingers like a vice through her coat sleeve. 'Let me go!' she managed to say, prising uselessly at his fingers.

'I still might have this whole incident opened up. Your answers are by no means satisfactory,' he replied grimly, all vestige of humour gone now, so that her first sneaking suspicion that he was merely giving her a hard time for the perverse pleasure it gave him was swept aside.

She flung back her head, platinum-blonde spikes brushing his chin, and he flinched back as if he expected her to hit him with her free hand, but his grip tightened and she stamped her foot in frustration.

'Wild little thing, aren't you?' he murmured close to her ear. 'Now, tell me who sent you.'

'Nobody sent me! How many times do I have to tell you?'

'Then what in hell were you playing at?'

'I've already told you. I thought I could pay——' She broke off.

'So how much could you have actually put on the counter?' he asked grimly.

'I suppose you intend to open the whole

thing up?' She dropped her gaze. This was awful. She was always getting into scrapes of some sort, but she could usually brazen her way out. Now she just felt silly and naïve. 'I could have paid if they accepted normal money!' She raised her voice. 'I guess I could outbid *you* any day!' She flung her head back again, but was still unable to make any impression on the iron hold with which he held her arm. 'You de Maines are small fry where I come from,' she boasted. 'All I have to do is go to along to an Express office first thing in the morning. I didn't know I had to have the money in my actual hand. It's primitive!'

'I'm curious to know how much you've rooked me for,' he said, ignoring her outburst. 'How much could you lay down now?'

'I—I don't know.' The few pounds in sterling burned in her pocket. She must have cost him nearly two thousand if they were playing by the book.

'Oh, hell.' He suddenly let her go and for a moment they stood next to each other, too close for ordinary conversation—and too distant, came the renegade thought into Goldie's head, to be taken in his arms . . .

As if aware of what was in her mind, he moved back and straddled a wooden chair. 'I've just realised who you are,' he said in a dull, flat voice. 'I always forget Ravella is older than she looks. She'll be forty now. That makes her old enough to be your mother.' He gave another of the grim smiles that made the hollows beneath the jutting cheekbones deepen. 'Of course, your mother didn't give you instructions to come along and bid up. Of course not,' he added sarcastically.

'Of course she didn't!' Goldie bit back. 'Why on earth would she do that?'

'Why?' Teeth flashed in the weather-tanned expanse of his face as he gave a derisive laugh. 'She always likes to throw the cat among the pigeons, doesn't she?' He chuckled almost admiringly, then a thought seemed to strike him. 'I suppose she guesses the proceeds of the sale will go to her eventually, too?'

Goldie looked at him, too stunned to speak. 'Actually,' she told him, 'she doesn't know I'm here. And if she did, she wouldn't give a damn about a single stick here—or what they've fetched. She's got so much money she doesn't know what to do with it. A few thousand here or there won't make a blind bit of difference. I came along because I would have liked the painting. It means a lot to me. And I really can't see why you should go to all this trouble to get it. It's not exactly Rembrandt.'

'It's a very nice painting.'

'Two thousand pounds nice?'

He smiled then, without rancour. 'You're an expensive little thing. I feel you owe me.'

She held her breath. This was where he made a pass. It was amazing how rapidly he'd got to the point, especially after the way they'd started out. Country hick or not, he was as smooth an operator as anybody she'd met.

He gave a soft chuckle. 'No, sweetheart. You can't read me like a book. I wasn't going to ask that.' The bark-brown eyes flecked over her pink face. 'You're not exactly my type. Though with a nice sensible hair-do and some decent clothes you could look quite presentable.' Then he added insultingly, 'If you dressed with more decorum, perhaps you wouldn't invite the response from men you're so obviously expecting.'

To stem the rising tide of her anger, she switched on her iciest manner. 'You're wasting my time. I can't stand here bandying words; I've got to go. But,' here curiosity got the better of her, 'I think you owe me an answer to one question.'

He raised his eyebrows.

Despite her actress's training, she couldn't control the way her lips tightened with renewed disappointment at what had happened. 'Why on earth,' she asked, 'did you want that painting so badly?'

CHAPTER TWO

A GUARDED look had come into his face, and he must have had luck on his side, too, because at the same moment there was a commotion in the corridor and the door was opened cautiously to allow a short, portly looking man in a dark blue suit and college tie to come in.

'I say, are you the chap who just bought the Halliwell?' He addressed Goldie's adversary, but his eyes kept straying to her, especially to her legs, and she felt her animosity direct itself equally between the two men. It was her cue to leave. She cut across the room and was nearly at the door before a figure bulked in the way.

'Look, I—er . . .' he glanced back at the newcomer, one hand indicating Goldie '. . . I'm in conference, actually, old chap.' He smiled accommodatingly. 'So sorry . . .'

'I say, I do beg your pardon.' The stranger gave a knowing smile, but despite his apology for barging in he dived straight on with what he'd wanted to ask anyway. 'The thing is, I think I've probably got a purchaser for it, if you're willing to sell on?' He raised his

26

eyebrows in expectation.

'Again, I have to say sorry,' replied Goldie's captor, for by this time he was gripping her firmly by the elbow. 'My client will be most unwilling to sell—at any price,' he added.

'Here's my card,' the man said, feeling in his pocket for his wallet and extracting a white card which he pushed towards them. 'Just in case. It looks as if I missed all the fun,' he went on conversationally. 'Didn't realise there was going to be anything big. You never can tell with these country sales. Lunching, don't you know? Nice little restaurant down the road. Still, bear me in mind, old chap. Bear me in mind.'

As Goldie was almost half out of the door, though prevented from making a complete escape by the hand round her elbow, it seemed natural on this note for Goldie and Mr de Maine to make some kind of farewell. They both had the same idea at the same moment, and she found herself being hustled out into the corridor. Before she could make sense of what was happening a voice called, 'Lucas! So there you are!'

An elegantly dressed woman of about fifty, with white hair that looked rather striking against a deeply tanned face, left the group she was talking to and came towards them. 'Did you get what you wanted?'

'I always do, Violet.'

'I must say,' she swept on, 'you went wild over poor Brendan's little painting.' She gave Goldie a quick, appraising, not overtly critical look, but one lacking in warmth, and went on, 'I've got some of Eva's wonderful old evening dresses. I couldn't bear the thought of them sliding down the scale until they finished up in some jumble sale or worse. Hugh's just taking them out to the car for me.'

Lucas, thought Goldie. Lucas de Maine. She'd never heard of a Lucas. Or had she? Burgh Hall had always been peopled by oldies. At twelve, that had meant anybody over twenty. But she vaguely remembered a son or two. Much older than she was, or they had seemed so at that time. They had been away at school, and in the holidays the whole family had decamped to Italy. Some villa. Something which, at that time, had seemed unbelievably exotic.

'Are you coming back, then?' There was an impatient edge to her voice now, as Lucas apparently failed to respond.

Goldie noticed that his hand had slipped discreetly away from her elbow. Feeling that this was the opportunity she wanted, she started to walk on towards the front door. Sun was beginning to stream in through the stained glass now that the rain had stopped, and she paused for a moment with her hand on the brass knob, blues and reds and purples staining her skin. How many times had she stood in just this position in the past, regret at leaving filling her heart, or regret at being left behind? Now she felt a surge of something similar.

She turned back, intending just a quick glance over her shoulder. Lucas de Maine was standing gazing after her over the head of the white-haired woman who blocked his path. Their glances collided. Goldie felt her breath draw in. It was crazy. He was just a country man, a farmer presumably, or an estate agent, a vet—anything. But what was obvious from the clothes he wore was that their life-styles were totally dissimilar. Oil and water. Chalk and cheese. Sugar and salt. And she was 'not his type'. End of story.

She turned rapidly and pushed her way outside, running down the steps into the fresh air and beginning to walk away down the drive as fast as she could. It had been an expensive waste of time flying over here. A futile jaunt to satisfy some sentimental whim. Lost in thought, she didn't realise someone had called her name until she heard footsteps beside her on the gravel and felt a hand on her arm. It was Sam Woollard.

'Hetty meant it about tea, Goldie. She's gone on ahead to put the kettle on.'

'Oh, Sam . . .' She held him by the hand.

'I'd love to come.' She glanced back at the main door of Eva's rambling old house. Any minute a figure might appear in the doorway, but though she hesitated it stayed firmly shut.

Sam urged her down the drive. 'Ravella was always a favourite of Hetty's. Follows her career as if she's one of her own. She's over the moon to see you after all this time,' he told her.

'I remember making a real nuisance of myself over your apple trees,' admitted Goldie. Memory had blunted her recognition of the couple at first, but now, with the alteration of the passing years taken into account, she recalled Sam's reddish hair, now iron-grey, and the ample figure of his wife perpetually swathed in a flowered apron, and now so much slimmer and smarter. Of course, their children, almost grown up then, would have left home long ago by now, leaving the couple free to make something of themselves.

Together they strolled up the half-familiar drive. The trees bordering it had changed. They were bigger, bushier. But little else was different.

'It's so pretty. I'd forgotten, you know. It isn't easy to remember when you're jetting all over the place as I am.' They exchanged smiles before going inside.

Hetty was in the kitchen. 'Now then, Goldie, first things first. Where are you staying, love?'

'Actually, I haven't booked in anywhere yet. I was going to get a taxi back to Driffield and see if I could get in somewhere there.'

'Nonsense, lass. You'll stay here—won't she, Sam?'

'Just what I was going to suggest. Besides, you'll never get a taxi on a Saturday. And it would cost a fortune. Money wasted when you're welcome here. Eva would never have forgiven us if we let you go traipsing off! Besides,' he added, to clinch matters, 'Hetty's like a hen without any chicks just now. You'll be doing her a favour.'

Goldie stood helplessly in the kitchen doorway, clutching her shoulder-bag, the big coat sliding down off her shoulders again. She felt like a waif and stray being offered the hand of rescue. Suddenly she knew she wanted to stay more than anything else in the world. 'It's home, isn't it?' She blinked. 'You're so kind. I'd forgotten that.' She felt she'd forgotten a lot.

'The weekend, then. Longer, if you like. But we know you're busy. What are you in at the moment?' Hetty, beaming now, bustled about preparing tea.

'Well, we've just finished filming in

Columbia, and I'm scheduled to start another in the summer. I've got a nice long rest ahead of me. Nearly four months.' She'd decided to spend four months working on herself. Change of diet. Change of gym. Change of acting classes. Change of apartment—maybe give up the flat altogether and stay in the mountains somewhere, living simply off the land. Take up yoga again, really get into herself and discover what it was she really wanted. It sounded good; she couldn't wait to start. It was just that it also sounded lonely.

She helped Hetty sort out the cups and saucers and they chatted amiably together, reminding each other of acquaintances from the past. Hetty told her she had five grandchildren now, with another due any day, and Goldie asked after the names she remembered, friends she'd always taken up with whenever she had been shunted off to Aunty Eva's, as she'd called her when she was little. Her friends had either married and settled in the district, or gone away for good as she had herself.

'If I'd been older than twelve I would have kept in touch properly, but at that age, and going to Hollywood of all places, one thinks only of the future,' she explained when they were sitting down in front of a roaring fire. Her bone-china plate had its rose pattern almost obliterated by the huge slab of fruitcake Hetty had placed on it. Looking at it, Goldie gulped. 'I'd forgotten Yorkshire teas, too,' she smiled. 'I think I'm going to put on weight!'

'You could do with it, there's nowt on you,' observed Sam, not unkindly.

There was a knock at the door. 'I'll get it.' Hetty rose to her feet. 'Now, you pour us all another cup of tea, Sam. I won't be a tick.'

Goldie heard voices in the hall. She was just reaching out to hand her empty cup to Sam when Hetty came back in. Turning, she nearly dropped her saucer. There was Lucas de Maine, smiling broadly and looking most unlike a man who had just had to pay one and a half thousand pounds over the odds for something.

'Afternoon, Sam,' he greeted his host in the laconic manner of the region. Without being invited, he sat down beside Goldie on the sofa. She felt his thigh against her own. With her eyes steadily on the teapot which Sam was upending into her cup, she tried to pretend that Lucas had called to see the Woollards. But she knew it wasn't true. There was something cracklingly alive about him. It was as if his whole body, pressing so dangerously against her own, were vibrating with electricity. And she knew that she was the cause of it.

'Goldie's staying for the weekend,' began Hetty, taking the teapot from Sam and automatically going through into the kitchen to refill it and bring in an extra cup and saucer for Lucas.

'That'll be convenient,' remarked Lucas to Goldie.

She pretended she didn't know he was looking at her. 'Will it?' she asked.

'Lucas has the millhouse for now,' Sam informed her. The millhouse was over the road from the Woollards' on de Maine land.

'I thought you'd be living at Burgh Hall,' she blurted before she could stop herself. It was nothing to her where he lived. Now he would think she was interested.

'Time enough for Burgh Hall when Uncle drops off the twig,' he said bluntly. 'I'll be there for keeps, then.'

'I'm not surprised you moved out so sharp,' observed Sam. 'Coming out of the Army like you, he'd be doubly hard to take. I can't imagine Martin having anybody under the same roof as himself for long. He was an awkward devil when he was younger, and he's worse now he's getting on.' He chuckled. 'It's to your credit he's still on friendly terms with you, Lucas.'

'He disinherits me regularly. One of these days he's going to kick the bucket when

I'm out of favour. It's worse than Russian roulette. But he's not so bad with a bit of careful handling. He's like my Queenie.'

Goldie thought he was referring to some girlfriend until Sam began to chuckle again. 'Aye, I heard you had a bit of a tumble the other day.'

'Bit stiff in the shoulder. Thought I was going to have to have it strapped up. I said to Harold, "Look, you've given Queenie a shot of something, what about me?" but he wasn't having any.' He turned to Goldie. 'Sorry about all this village gossip. Harold's the local vet.' His eyes were brilliant, almost black, and instead of turning away he simply looked at her, smiling. It was a challenging look, as if to underline the fact that he knew she thought they were all country yokels and he was playing up to it with his talk of vets and horses.

'Go ahead,' she said faintly, wondering what would happen next. In fact, she had quite enjoyed listening to them talk. Now he was so close that she could see the lines on either side of his eyes as he crinkled them up. His lashes were coal-black and his skin had that lovely, firm, healthy look of somebody who spent a lot of time outdoors. The thought made her ask, 'I suppose you farm the de Maine estates?' Collecting pictures must be a hobby.

'I suppose I do,' he replied, averting his glance.

'Sam,' he said, 'I know you all think I was a bit hotheaded this afternoon, but I didn't even get through the front door before somebody was asking me to sell the Halliwell on. What do you make of that?'

'You know about these things. Don't ask me how. Must have taught you more in the Army than they did in my day.'

'He was a dealer,' Lucas went on to explain. 'He's seen me around at salerooms now and then. Part of a ring. I've always steered clear of him.'

'How's that part going, then?'

'Very well. It's really taken off. I guess people realise they can trust me.'

Goldie was mystified and looked it, but nobody bothered to explain. As they talked she wondered when Lucas would get around to admitting why he was here. There was obviously some reason up his sleeve. She remembered him saying she owed him, and wondered if he still thought that. Although he gave every appearance of being a man sitting at ease, with his legs stretched out towards the fire and a teacup and saucer and some of Hetty's slab cake balanced beside him on a plate, she could feel the tension in him. At any moment he would explode.

Eventually he said he'd better be going.

'Hugh and Violet think I'm not eating properly, so they've invited me to dinner.' He smiled down at Goldie. 'You'll see me out, won't you?'

'Can't you find your own way? I'm hardly the person to ask.' She scowled. It was making her nervy, sitting next to him while he boiled and steamed with some inner heat that was practically scouring the surface of her skin.

He pulled her up beside him as he rose, and a quick glance at Sam and Hetty showed her that they fully approved. But then they had always been partisan in their affections—not many people had been on Ravella's side. Even at twelve, Goldie had known that. The cool encounter with the woman Goldie now remembered as Violet had brought back memories of the same response in other folk. She remembered that particular coldness when they had mentioned Ravella, or referred to 'Ravella's child'.

When they reached the door and were out of earshot of the older couple, Goldie turned to him. 'You shouldn't have done this. They'll think you're interested.'

'I am.'

'Much good may it do you. I leave on Monday.' She hadn't made any decision, but it was as well to get the record straight.

'That gives me two evenings and one full

day to get you to change your mind and stay longer.'

'Lucas!' His name came naturally to her and she was about to remonstrate, taking him at his word, when she thought she caught a gleam in his eye that might have been humour. She bit her lip, angry at having been caught out. Damn it, she'd wanted him to want her to stay!

'Well, if I do decide to stay on and have a short holiday,' she said stiffly, 'I hope you won't go thinking it's because I'm interested in you!'

'Might you stay on?' he asked, eyes sharpening.

'I don't know. I don't have any plans. That's how I like it.'

'Lucky you to have the choice.' He shrugged, not smiling, and opened the door. 'I was exaggerating, anyway, I wouldn't be able to work my charm on you tonight, because I've promised Hugh and Violet.' He gave her a lingering, up and down look. 'I'd take you along with me, but I can just imagine Violet's face if I walked in with someone looking like you.'

She gasped.

'I'm sorry. I didn't mean to be hurtful.' He looked concerned when he saw her expression. 'No need to take it to heart. We're blunt round here. I thought you would remember that. You spent your formative years here, didn't you?'

'Blunt or not, it's a horrible thing to say.' She must have got him completely wrong—she really had thought he was interested, despite him saying she wasn't his type. There was no other explanation for his unexpected visit here. But obviously she'd jumped to the wrong conclusion.

'Dear Violet prefers the conventional type,' he went on to explain, 'the type I'm supposed to install as lady of Burgh Hall. Not even you would claim you fit the bill there, would you?'

She curled her lip, but before she could utter another word he said abruptly, 'See you later.' He was down the steps and half-way along the drive before she recovered. She watched as he reached the gate. When he got there he swung left across the lane without even glancing back.

Hmm, she thought. It was the only comment that came to mind. What on earth was she to make of him? Returning to the sitting-room she was conscious of Hetty's satisfaction at seeing Lucas de Maine flirting in public. Matchmaking, she remembered, had always been a favourite topic of Eva's and her mother's.

'Where's the rest of your luggage, Goldie?' asked Sam as she helped Hetty clear away.

'That's all I brought,' she said, indicating

the flight bag in the doorway. 'I hate queueing for baggage, so I always squeeze whatever I'm going to need into a bag I can take on board with me. When I get to the other end I buy anything I really need.' It was also part of her new aim to start living simply. Sam didn't say anything, but she knew he, too, thought her clothes outlandish and not at all smart.

She went upstairs with Hetty and was shown into a pretty blue and white bedroom. It looked out over the garden at the very apple trees she used to climb against all orders when she was a child. They'd grown somewhat, and one of them had had to have a wooden support fixed under it.

Later she helped Hetty prepare an evening meal. By the time they had eaten she was already feeling sleepy, and was glad Hetty and Sam would be turning in soon after ten o'clock. If nothing else, she could catch up on her sleep this weekend.

Soon, cocoa-mug in hand, she went upstairs. It had been cosy sitting round the fire after Hetty's excellent cooking and chatting about local matters, and she yawned comfortably, hearing Sam put the chain across the front door after settling the dogs in the yard. She waited until the bathroom was free, then went along to have a quick shower and clean her teeth. Then, ready for bed, she climbed in and switched out the light. A few minutes later she was almost asleep when a sound at the window disturbed her.

Turning over, she was just about to drift off again when it came a second time. It was a rattling sound against the glass. Like a bird pecking . . . or a shower of small stones. She sat bolt upright. There was a pause. Then again, the same sound.

Anticipating trouble, she leaped quickly out of bed and crossed the room, pushing back the curtains until she could peer down into the garden. It was pitch-black outside, but when her eyes became accustomed to the dark she could just make out a blur on the grass which she couldn't account for. It moved. And again there was a shower of something pattering against the glass.

Gravel. Somebody was throwing gravel! And there could only be one answer to the question who. Edging the window open, she whispered down as loudly as she dared, conscious of Sam and Hetty asleep across the landing.

'Who is it?'

'Come on, you're not asleep. Get dressed and come out for a drink before closing time.'

'Don't be ridiculous. I'm in bed.'

'Want me to come up and join you?'

'For goodness' sake, Lucas!'

'Come on down, then. Put any old thing on; we'll go to the Coach and Horses.' He named the pub on the village green.

'I can't.' She searched for a reason. 'It's a crazy idea,' she said lamely.

'It's an excellent idea. I thought of it half-way through dinner, and couldn't wait to come and tell you. And, anyway, if you don't come down this instant, I promise I'll wake everyone up—including the dogs,' he added darkly.

They're supposed to be guard dogs, she thought crossly to herself as she closed the window with care and went over to her bed. It looked very inviting. But she had no doubt that Lucas would carry out his threat.

She started to fumble around in her bag for something to put on. It wouldn't hurt to have a little drink, she supposed. But what to wear? Her other clothes were in a heap on the floor, and somewhat travel-stained. All she had was a mini-shift in white silk. Heavens knew why she was so impractical when it came to packing for herself. Probably because the studios always took good care of her appearance. Now she slithered into the shift, not bothering with a bra or slip, simply pulling on a clean pair of panties and tights. It would have to be the ankle boots again. And the same coat. She would keep it pulled tightly around her, and nobody need ever know what she had on underneath. She just knew what it would be like at the Coach and Horses. All men. All dressed in identical tweeds. Darts. Dominoes. Country talk. She would be the only woman there. The whole idea was mad. But she couldn't help smiling as she crept quietly down the stairs. Lucas was extraordinary. He looked so conventional, yet here he was throwing gravel at windows. She wondered if he made a habit of it.

CHAPTER THREE

'YOU realise this is blackmail?' she demanded as she let herself out through the front door to find him waiting for her in the porch.

'Of course it is. Everyone has their price. I knew I'd got you when I mentioned the dogs.'

'Lucas de Maine——'

'Shush, sound carries at night—and anyway, they'll be calling last orders soon, so there's no time for talk.' Contrary to what he had said, he talked all the way as he tucked her hand in his and made her jog-trot along the pitch-black country lane towards the village. He told her how boring it had been at dinner, and how he couldn't wait to get away, and he did a hilarious imitation of another couple Violet had invited, whose sole topic of conversation had been the price of houses. He had wondered if she'd been as bored as he had, having to make polite conversation when she'd rather have been with him.

Before she could make some scathing reply to cut him down to size, he went on, 'Then it struck me what a good idea it would be if we both finished off with a night-cap here.

Actually,' he added as they reached the door, 'once we're in, we're safe for an hour or two. After last orders Bert locks up and switches the lights off in the front parlour, and everyone repairs to the saloon bar at the back. Good,' he poked his head round the door, 'just made it.'

This was another thing Goldie had forgotten. Brief trips back to the UK after she'd reached the age to drink in bars had included one or two village pubs, though not this one. She'd forgotten the Saturday night frenzy as people tried to drink enough in the time allotted. Contrary to expectations, though, this wasn't a place full of old men playing dominoes. Everyone was well under thirty—the age at which she began to write people off as has-beens—and there seemed to be some kind of party going on.

When she hung back he said, 'Don't be silly. It's always like this. I know most of them—I was at school with three-quarters of the chaps. Just ignore them. We'll find a quiet corner.' He settled her in an ingle-nook and went to the bar. Judging by the response he got, he hadn't been boasting when he'd said he knew everyone. And he was obviously well-liked. Goldie felt a twinge of envy to think there was nowhere apart from the studio she could go where she would get this sort of treatment. If people did come up to her in restaurants, it was only because she was the daughter of a star and they could tell their friends they'd spoken to her. Here it was all so natural. People greeted Lucas because they liked him.

He confirmed this obliquely when he returned. 'Take no notice of what anybody says,' he told her. 'They'll tease you unmercifully for sitting here with me. It's known as lovers corner. They've been trying to get me to sit in it for years.'

He put out a hand. 'Don't get up, idiot. You can handle this crowd, can't you? Look,' he went on, 'they're only old schoolfriends. That guy over there, you see?' She followed his glance. 'He was great at rugby—school captain. He now farms Lea Holme. Remember that?'

She frowned.

'Big, old white house at the head of the valley. Beautiful land. And the chap next to him owns one of the best shoots around, up on the moors at Scardale. And that other guy—his old man's a high court judge, and Ruan's all set to follow in his footsteps. Looks as if he's laying down the law to somebody now. And that bearded guy coming over to us is—Harold! Just warning her off you,' he said as a young man with a full black beard leaned confidentially towards them.

He addressed Goldie directly. 'You've got

some stiff competition, be warned. Goes by the name of Queenie.' He winked. 'Give him the boot and come with me. I'm a much better bet.'

'Just go away, Harold. He's a vet,' he said to Goldie. 'Keep well clear. Harold,' he said, turning back, 'I'm trying to have a tête-à-tête with this lovely young visitor to our shores, so will you please remove yourself? And you might warn the clods over there to keep away, too,' he added as Harold, grinning broadly, walked over to join another crowd.

'You are lucky, Lucas. It's like having a large, happy family.'

'I don't know about happy. But I know what you mean about family. As laird designate I suppose I do regard them as family.'

'As what?' She looked at him curiously.

He frowned. 'All this tommy-rot about being lord of the manor. Burgh Hall has been the manor house since the year dot. We built this village, for heaven's sake. Put it on the map. Boring, isn't it?'

'I think it's fascinating.'

'Now I know you're American.'

'I didn't think I'd got any kind of accent.'

'I didn't mean the accent.' His eyes sharpened and she thought he was going to go on, but instead he simply looked thoughtful.

'I don't really belong anywhere,' she went

on, not trying to work out what that look had meant, 'so I don't cultivate an accent. I worked it out long ago. An accent is a bit like the clothes you choose. It shows which club you want to belong to. Usually people fit in with their background. Like you,' she added. 'Your voice is just so upper-class English, you would just have to wear the clothes you do and live in a place like this.'

'You find it quaint, I suppose?'

She looked surprised. 'No. It's real. It's very—solid.'

'Like a well-made film set?'

She laughed. 'You sound serious.'

'I'm always serious, Goldie.' She caught the look in his eye and this time there was no ambiguity.

'You know it's no good,' she said, feeling uncomfortably aware of how close they were forced to sit in the nook.

He ran his little finger up the inside of her wrist under the cover of her sleeve. She felt it make little whorls on her suddenly responsive skin.

'Please, don't.'

'I can't help it.'

She snatched her hand away and pushed it into her pocket. 'I don't like being played with.'

'Who's playing?' His lips were close to her ear, but there was nowhere to move to, and something other than physical constraint held her chained in position. She felt his breath, warm, teasing her earlobe. Then his lips were brushing lightly, almost as if by accident, against the side of her cheek. He moved away and reached for his drink. 'Maybe this lovers' seat wasn't a good idea,' he murmured. 'I don't think I'm going to be able to keep my hands off you.'

'I'm tired, actually. I think I'd like to go back after this drink.'

He didn't reply, but they lingered a little longer, keeping up a pretence of conversation, though all the while underneath Goldie was aware of something else fermenting. It was fizzing away like champagne, and she wondered if it would explode as soon as they got outside. And whether she could handle it. Him. Her own unexpected emotions.

'You didn't tell me why the painting by Brendan Halliwell was so important to you,' she reminded him, hoping this was a fairly neutral topic by now.

'It isn't particularly. It's important to my client,' he informed her abruptly.

'Client?' she queried.

'I do a little buying and selling now and then,' he admitted, as if it was something to be ashamed of. 'I have to earn a living somehow.'

'I thought you had the estate?' she asked,

surprised.

'You did, did you?'

'Well,' she frowned, not able to read the expression on his face, 'that's what I *thought*.'

There was no expression on his face as he explained, 'The estate is run by a very efficient team of professionals. Certainly I'm involved. But I don't draw an income from it yet. That won't come until Uncle Martin goes, God bless him. In the meantime he keeps me on a very small stipend. That's the way it's always been,' he added, to forestall what he obviously thought was going to be an exclamation about how unfair it was. 'He rather looks down on my dealing. Calls it a lot of arty nonsense. Luckily I can ride and shoot, so he hasn't lost all faith in me. And, as I tell him, one has to earn one's crust somehow. Actually, I do well enough, though I'd hate to have to go on dealing forever. It would be soul-destroying. You see, when you said you could top my bid, personally you were right. You've probably got ten times as much of a personal fortune as I have. Do you want to go now?'

'What? Now?' Taken aback by the suddenness of the question, she shook her head. Then her face broke into a smile. 'Oh, I see. You think I'm after your millions! And, now you've told me the horrid truth, you think I want to run out? Let me remind you, Lucas de Maine, it was you who came round to my bedroom window with your pockets full of gravel.'

'So maybe I'm after your millions?' His lips brushed her hair. 'You do see why I'm not free to do what I want, don't you?' His tone told her he was being deadly serious. 'I could be well into middle age before I have an income worth having. Not a good marriage prospect, as any girl would agree.'

'You sound as if you're talking from bitter experience.' She laughed, but her smile died when she saw his expression.

'Let's go and talk about this somewhere else,' he suggested, his expression teasing once again.

'Lucas, you've trapped me here. How can I get home in safety with you as my escort?' Suddenly she did feel geniunely afraid. Not of him, but of herself. She ached with wanting him. Ever since they had had that run in after the auction, she had felt a physical pain in the pit of her stomach. Now, as he circled his fingers inside her palm, she knew what it was.

'You know I'm a gentleman, Goldie. You'll find me boringly easy to handle.'

She gave a disbelieving laugh. He only had to look at her with those teasing dark eyes for her common sense to desert her.

Before they got up he asked suddenly, 'Why

"Goldie"? Is it a nickname?'

'No. It was my mother's whim. She was a bit of a hippy before she made a name for herself after I was born. She thought it amusing to choose the most outlandish name she could find. It's from some book or other on meditation, short for Goldenblossom. As it had to be shortened, I thought Goldie sounded marginally better than Blossom.'

He exploded with laughter. 'I'm so sorry. I shouldn't laugh. But isn't that Ravella all over? She's priceless, isn't she? The darling.'

'You knew her? In person, I mean?' People often talked as if they knew her mother, but it was usually no more than a screen acquaintance.

'Of course I did.' He frowned. 'It was only ten years ago when you left. I was an innocent sixteen-year-old.' He laughed. 'First Brendan, then Willett, then Martin, of all people, then me.'

'What do you mean?' She recognised the names. They were all the de Maine men. Willett must have been Lucas's father.

'Her lovers, ex-lovers, and faithful servants.'

'You mean my mother? You're actually talking about my mother? But she's years older than you.'

'What's age got to do with it?' He grinned

disarmingly. 'I followed her around like a dog all one summer. Where were you, by the way?'

'That must have been the summer I was sent to learn French.' She frowned. 'This is outrageous, Lucas. I thought you were so conventional. I mean, she must have been thirty, and——'

'I wasn't her lover, if that's what you're thinking. I was the faithful servant. I don't think she knew I existed. She was far too involved with Martin.'

'I didn't know that.'

'I expect there's a lot you don't know about your mother,' he added, grinning at her anxious frown. 'All water under the bridge, though, isn't it?' He rose to his feet and pulled her up beside him, causing her coat to fall open. The dark eyes acquired a predatory gleam. 'I say—I wondered what you had on underneath that coat. I suspected pyjamas, but it looks like a cute little nightie.'

'I'll have you know this is a designer dress in pure silk, and it cost——'

'Far more than I'll ever be able to afford,' he said with a scowl. 'Come on, let's go.'

A chorus of goodnights and advice on how to handle him followed them out, and but for the strange switch-about in his moods and her own fizzing emotions tossing her all ways it would have been a perfect end to the day.

Now, as they set off across the green, she wondered if either of them could guess how things were going to end.

When they gained the path leading back towards the house he had one arm round her waist already. She half turned, intending to ask him to take it away, but instead she blurted, 'You're not so tall, after all.' Her face was almost level with his chin.

'Just under six feet. If you take off those little high-heeled boots you might change your tune.' His tone was light.

He could easily take me in his arms now, she thought. But he didn't. Instead he turned and started to walk on down the narrow path.

She caught up with him and slipped her arm through his. 'You treat me like a child, don't you?' she challenged, thinking of what he had said about her mother and wondering if all his teasing merely covered the fact that he preferred older women. The thought made her miserable. 'I'm twenty-two,' she told him. 'You're not much older. Closer to my generation than——' she paused '—than anything,' she added lamely.

'What's age got to do with it?' he asked again. But this time his voice was husky, and suddenly he stopped dead in the lane and said hurriedly, 'I'm trying to keep you at a distance, Goldie. Can't you tell? Don't come near me, or I won't be responsible.'

'Don't you come near me!' she said, as he reached out for her despite his words.

'That's like saying don't obey the law of gravity.'

'Well, don't then!' she retorted, despite the fact that he was pulling her towards him and she wasn't resisting in the slightest.

'I'd have to be an astronaut not to—come to think of it, maybe that's what it is—I feel like a moon-walker. Nothing's like it usually is. I've never felt like this before. You're driving me wild—with exasperation, I mean—but instead of making me want to forget you, it makes me want to do something entirely different . . .' He paused. His voice was mesmerisingly soft, and when it trailed to a deep whisper she involuntarily moved closer, lips parted, to hear what he said next.

'You look,' he murmured, 'like an angel from heaven . . .' Before she could say anything his lips closed sweetly over hers. It was no good fighting. She didn't want to fight, anyway. He was powerful and she could feel his will reaching out, drawing her closer than touching till all her thoughts were in a chaos of confusion, with only the one obvious one thrusting its eventual way to the top.

Despite the heat of his embrace, she couldn't help shivering. Her feeling for him was drawing her into a strange web of old loves and intrigues. Brendan and Ravella. Willett and Ravella. Lucas and Ravella . . . And now Lucas and Goldie.

She felt his lips lift fractionally, and she realised that he was looking at her through the darkness.

'I can feel your mind racing round with all its little cogs and ratchets whirring along nineteen to the dozen,' he said. 'I know what you're thinking.'

'Oh, yes?' She rather hoped not.

'You're thinking, he's shooting me a line, but I'm determined to keep on saying no; or, because you're not very sure of yourself just now, you're thinking, maybe he really means it, so how do I extricate myself without hurting his feelings?'

'You mean I'm thinking two opposite things?' she asked, stalling to give herself time to work it out.

'If it's any consolation,' he went on, 'I'm thinking half a dozen opposite things, too—though most of them have us ending up in bed,' he added frankly.

She pushed at him, suddenly reluctant to be in his arms if all it came down to was bed.

'I'm glad you admit your interest is only carnal!' she bit out.

'I didn't admit anything of the sort,' he told

her, drawing her unresisting body back so that it was aligned with his again. 'But admit it, the thought has crossed your mind. And, at a guess, you're as confused as I am.'

'I'm confused, yes.' She buried her head against his coat for a moment. One of his hands came up and stroked the nape of her neck. 'I've seen what happens when people get involved. And when you say you were in love with my mother——'

'I didn't say that. I said I was her faithful servant. She was the epitome of womanhood to me in those days—warm and beautiful and sexy . . . I didn't count fidelity as a virtue then. Lack of it seemed far more fun. It was part of the package, and the price you paid for loving dangerously. Goldie,' his tone changed, 'doesn't it seem too much like fate that you should be here with me?'

'It's still no good, is it? We come from two different worlds.' Despite her protest, she felt something inside give in, only her head still struggled against her heart. 'And I've seen what happens to love.'

'With someone you could trust it would be different.'

'But how can we trust anyone? It's not people's own fault they fall out of love. Feelings can't be helped. That's how they work—beyond control.' She knew it now. It was happening to her against all expectations, and it made her struggle harder against it. 'I daren't base my life on feelings, Lucas. And I certainly daren't base it on anybody else's feelings.'

'Deadlock.'

She nodded.

'But everybody has to risk love some time. You can't put the shutters up.'

'I don't want to risk it,' she told him stubbornly.

He held her close. 'You're confused, and, if it's any comfort, so am I. As I said, I feel like somebody in outer space—nothing's solid any more. All the old certainties seem useless.' He hesitated, and then he said, 'Obviously I can never marry you.'

She raised her head.

'We're so very different. As you said, we come from different worlds and it just wouldn't work. And then Martin would disinherit me for sure. It's not just your crazy clothes,' he added, 'but you're Ravella's daughter. There's no way round that.'

'You're thinking further ahead than me. I was only thinking about going to bed with you.'

'You were?' He mimed an expression of lecherous interest.

'Oh, Lucas, don't be such a fool. I didn't mean I was actually thinking about it, as such, I mean—oh, what do I mean?' She moved angrily away, taking him by surprise so that it was easy to slip out of his grasp. 'It's no good, is it? I thought we were just playing with each other, flirting in a sort of light-hearted way, but——' Suddenly she felt like crying. It didn't make sense. Nothing did. She felt so desolate all of a sudden. Alone and confused.

'Here.' He gave her a hug, then began kissing the top of her head, saying, 'It can't be helped. It's just bad luck that we want each other so much.'

They walked on. Bad luck, he called it. She couldn't think straight, but bad luck wasn't in it. For her it seemed bigger than that. As if destiny itself had brought them deliberately together, and was just as deliberately pushing them apart.

It was extraordinary that they could be talking of marriage already, even if it was only to say it was out of the question. But it seemed the most natural thing in the world. What would it be like next week when she was back in Hollywood? They would probably scarcely remember each other's names. Which simply proved she was right. Feelings were wayward things, and best forgotten when it came to the important life decisions.

'Lucas. I don't know what's happening to me. I'm out of my depth. I've never been involved with anyone in a sort of romantic way like this.'

They had reached the gate by now and he walked up the drive to the house with her. It was beginning to rain again, drops pattering on the leaves of the shrubbery with a hundred soft little slaps.

'Involved?' he asked, raising his eyebrows. He looked out across the garden as if not sure what to do next.

'Come inside for a minute,' she said, wondering what Sam and Hetty would think if they knew she was inviting a man into the house at this time of night, even though it was one of the de Maines.

They stood together in the sitting-room with their coats on.

'Listen,' he said, when she switched on a light and they blinked at each other in the glare, 'there's no reason why we shouldn't see each other while you're around. We might have fallen for each other, but there's nothing to stop us fighting it together. We can help each other get over it.'

Goldie wasn't sure she wanted to help him stop wanting her—if he really did—but she couldn't tell him that. What she wanted was to stay in his arms forever. She sighed. In real life it wouldn't work. They both knew that. It was decent of him to have set the record straight at once. For different reasons, there was no future in it for either of them. Marriage was the only possible direction for her and, as he so rightly asked, could she see herself at Burgh Hall? No way.

'I'm glad you're so straightforward, Lucas. I've never felt like this before. I suppose it'll fade when I go back home.' And she added, 'It must be hell to care for somebody who's absolutely indifferent to you.'

He turned away, thrusting his hands into his pockets, standing by the window and looking out on to the black garden so that she couldn't see his expression.

'I'd better go up for a minute and do my hair,' she said to his back. 'Do you want a drink?'

He swung round and she caught sight of a bleak expression, making him look older and somehow world-weary, but he brought a smile to his lips as his eyes flicked over her. 'Your hair!' he mocked. 'Its little spikes are drooping.'

'It's from where you were running your hands through it,' she muttered, turning away. She wondered why she had had the misfortune to catch that look on his face when she'd made that stupid remark about the hell of loving somebody who was indifferent. It was obvious the memory of a past love-affair had been going through his mind. He must have had lots.

Before she went out he called her back. 'I'd better go now, so don't bother with a drink.

But let's plan our campaign. We could do it over lunch tomorrow.'

'What campaign?'

He flashed a smile. 'Our fight against this rather inconvenient attraction we feel for each other. I'm serious,' he went on. 'I mean, I guess I've really fallen for you. Attraction of opposites and all that. Obviously you've got to help me fight it. Maybe if you wear some of your really tasteless Hollywood-movie-star clothes and—well, you know, rattle on all through lunch about showbiz trivia, maybe then I'll be able to get over you?'

She lifted her head. 'Good idea, Lucas. And you can come along in your horrible tweeds and bore me to death with lots of hunting, shooting and fishing stories. Do that, and I guess we'll both be screaming to get away from each other.'

'It's a pact. In league against love! Twelve o'clock, then? I'll call for you in the farm vehicle.'

She nodded, vaguely wondering what the farm vehicle was. 'If it's a tractor, that'll put me off. I like good cars, sleek sports models for preference.'

As she put the chain across, after he'd left with only the briefest of goodnight kisses, she had plenty on her mind—not least the questions he had raised about exactly what had taken place that summer ten years ago. Had his role of faithful servant been as innocent as he made out? And what had her mother felt, having the sixteen-year-old Lucas following her about? She felt doomed to live in the shadow of her mother for the rest of her days. Then again, she thought, as she tossed and turned in bed, what was she to make of Lucas's obvious attraction? They couldn't be more unalike. It was true he played the part of an English gentleman farmer to perfection, but what did he really feel in his heart of hearts?

She tossed and turned restlessly until daylight began to filter into the room.

CHAPTER FOUR

GOLDIE didn't feel that the white silk shift would be suitable for a pub lunch, so she spent what was left of Sunday morning, by the time she eventually woke up, rinsing out the T-shirt and mini-skirt in which she had arrived. To her annoyance, they didn't dry in time on the radiator in her room, and she was reluctant to ask Hetty to let her use the dryer in the kitchen on a Sunday, so she had to make do with the silk shift after all.

She had just finished getting ready when there was the sound of a motor in the drive, so, guessing it was Lucas, she went downstairs to the front door to greet him. Hetty was looking smug as she left, obviously feeling responsible for the young love as she would see it, blossoming beneath her very eyes.

'I see you're wearing your nightie again,' he greeted her, coming round the side of a mud-spattered Land Rover to help her up into the passenger seat.

'It might interest you to know that I didn't bring anything else with me, as I thought I could buy what I needed here. I'd forgotten how primitive this place is. It's not that the shops aren't open when reasonable people might want to do some shopping—there are simply no shops.' She glared at him as if holding him personally responsible for the state of things. She had wondered how he would greet her, and now she knew.

'I'll run you into Driffield tomorrow morning, if you like. You'll be able to get a change of clothing there. Though not,' he added, 'the exclusive designer stuff you're used to.'

'I hardly expected it,' she murmured as he climbed in beside her. 'But thanks for the offer. As I leave tomorrow, I won't be able to take you up on it.'

'Some urgent reason to go back?' he asked, switching the engine on and letting the wheels skid as he drove off fast down the drive.

'Not really,' she admitted.

'Then stay a little longer. Why not?'

'There's nothing to stay for,' she told him, looking at him out of the corner of her eye.

'You've been away for ten years. I would have thought there were lots of reasons to make more of a trip of it. Regard it as a sentimental journey into your childhood.' By now he was driving rapidly along the main road towards the motorway, and spoke almost absent-mindedly, with his mind on the traffic.

It wasn't the answer she had hoped for, and she frowned to herself. 'I'd need more of an incentive than that if I was going to change my plans,' she told him primly.

He reached out across the cab and took the hand that lay in her lap and gave it a squeeze. 'I'd give you an incentive if I wasn't driving,' he told her lecherously.

'But you don't mean it,' she replied, taking her hand away and looking out of the window. Last night's conversation ran through her mind again. 'You simply want me to help you lay some ghost from the past, don't you?' She turned to look at him.

The clean-cut profile was etched against the light, the way the sun slanted in making his cheekbones jut in harsh relief with light and shadow. His nose was pure Roman and the jaw strong, only his lips too full, spoiling the effect of classic good looks, but giving him an extra-sensual look that made her stomach turn over with desire.

He appeared to be considering her words carefully, or perhaps he was simply watching the traffic—she couldn't be sure—but, whichever, he didn't answer, and it wasn't until they pulled up shortly in the car park beside a half-timbered inn a few miles further on that he took up what she'd said.

Switching off the engine, he removed the key from the ignition, then turned to her. 'Are you serious? Do you really think that's why I wanted to see you again?'

She shrugged, too confused to play games.

He reached out towards her, running a finger slowly down the side of her face. 'So what about you? What's your excuse for being here?'

She bore the sweet torture of his touch without flinching. It was years of practice before the cameras that made it easy to wipe all emotion from her face. 'Perhaps I was just carried away by the romance of the place yesterday,' she told him expressionlessly. 'Merrie England, lord of the manor. It's so feudal. I half expect to find myself in a rose-coloured gown at the top of a tower, with a white knight serenading me from the back of a caparisoned charger.'

'I see.' He gave a lop-sided smile. 'I've never seen myself as living history before. Let's go and eat.' Before she could amend what she had said he had swung down, slammed his door, and was locking it before she could move. She struggled with the catch and jumped down just as he came round to help.

'They do quite decent grub here on a Sunday,' he told her in a brisk manner that gave her no chance to speak first, and then with a curt nod he was striding off across the gravel to the entrance. Annoyed at being expected to follow, and confused by the speed with which they had somehow got on to the wrong foot, she made her way slowly after him, making him wait with the door open as she picked her way around the puddles in her silver-heeled boots.

'You need a pair of good green wellingtons,' he observed when she at last drew level.

'No way.' She lifted her chin as she swept past. 'This is my style and I'm sticking to it.'

They were sitting down on opposite sides of a dark oak table in a secluded corner lit by red-shaded wall-lights when he gave another of those lop-sided smiles and said, 'We couldn't be more different, could we?'

Goldie wanted to scream at him to stop saying it. She knew it. Wasn't it obvious? But why did he have to harp on it? The thought was like a knife in her heart. Yet he admitted he found her attractive. Of course, she should take that in the spirit in which it was intended, as just an example of his old-world gallantry.

She blurted something about opposites sometimes being attracted.

'Attracted, yes.' He reached for her hand across the table. 'At least we're not so deeply involved that it'll be painful to stop. Listen,' he said, changing the subject completely, 'if you would like to stay on a few days, I can drive you down to London to catch your flight. I have to go to a sale at Sotheby's the day after tomorrow. You might even come with me. It's great fun. Not unlike horse-racing.'

She smiled. 'Horse-racing?'

'It's a gamble, isn't it?' His eyes sparked. 'One never knows whether one's going to hit the jackpot and come away with something really rather special, or,' he added meaningfully, 'do a nosedive and pay over the odds for something worthless.'

'I *am* sorry about yesterday,' she told him.

'I've torn yesterday from my diary,' he told her, his smile fading.

She closed her eyes. There he goes again, she thought. It was their meeting he was tearing from his diary. Can I take much more of this? she asked herself.

She tried to pull herself together. 'It would be fun to do London. I came straight through from Heathrow to King's Cross, and didn't see it this time. It must be two years since I was last there,' she told him brightly.

'I'm going down on Tuesday,' he told her. 'Early start.'

It seemed settled. They ordered then, Lucas suggesting she have the game pie, and while they waited for everything to arrive she asked him about the Army. 'How long were you in?' she asked.

Taking her by surprise, he replied, 'Eight

years.'

'But that must mean you've just come out?'

He shook his head. 'I've been out two years now.' And seeing her puzzled expression, he added, 'I ran away from school in the traditional manner and joined up at sixteen.' He smiled.

She did a rapid calculation and realised that he must have joined up that summer in which he had played the faithful servant to Ravella.

'I took the precaution of joining the family regiment,' he went on, oblivious to the line her thoughts had taken. 'It took some of the heat out of the situation as far as Dad was concerned. But after a few years it didn't seem very interesting, so I joined the special service. That *was* quite interesting for a time.' His eyes crinkled as he observed her surprise. 'You see,' he told her, 'I *have* been to the end of the lane and back.' He gazed off into the distance. 'Not many places I haven't been to, come to think of it. On balance, things are somewhat more peaceful here. Eventually I decided life was worth living after all, so it seemed a good idea to get back into civilian life.' He shrugged. 'There you are, my life on the back of a postage stamp.'

'I'm sure there's more to it than that.' All kinds of questions filled her imagination. Not least the one about the impulse that had led him to run away from school and join up. It must have been something pretty powerful. Like a broken heart, perhaps? It was hardly the sort of question she could ask without risking embarrassment, humiliation, ridicule, or all three.

'I'm glad you now think life's worth living,' she said in a small voice.

'It's very much worth living,' he said with obvious relish, the sensual lips parting to reveal a gash of white teeth. But he added enigmatically, 'Despite the sense of duty that sets one's limits.'

'You mean your inheritance?' she asked. 'Does that really limit you?'

He nodded. 'I've already told you about that.' She got the feeling he meant more than the financial limitations he had mentioned last night, but the waitress brought their order then, and by the time she had moved away the conversation had turned to something else.

'So we must have been in Hong Kong at about the same time?' he remarked after she'd given him as brief an outline of her career to date as he had with his. 'We've both done a bit of globe-trotting between us,' he concluded.

At least it was something in common, but Goldie couldn't help saying, 'I've done as much as I want for a while. I'd just like to stay one year in a place, so I could see it during the different seasons. I seem to have lived in a perpetual summer for the last ten years. What is winter like?'

'You'll find out if you stick around here.'

She shivered. Maybe it was the impending flight back to the States, the inevitable leave-taking ahead of her, but she felt nervy, chilled somehow. It would be winter in several senses if she stayed on—it was early days yet, but she sensed it would be a kind of winter of the heart to live here yet to be locked out of his life. He noticed her shiver and leaned forward to touch her arm.

'You're frozen. You should have known what to expect.'

With her mind on the hopelessness of her feelings for him, she could only think in double-meanings. 'How could I have known what to expect?' she murmured, looking directly into his eyes.

He registered her words with a raising of his eyebrows, and she was gratified to see that he was sensitive enough to have caught her meaning, but his words dashed her hopes when he said, 'Life isn't always predictable or fair. When it is, on those rare, wonderful occasions when everything seems to go just right, we should give thanks. The rest of the time there's no choice but to put on a brave face.'

She nodded, trying to bring a sophisticated smile to her lips to show that she, too, knew life was like that. Hollow laughter rose up, but she stifled it and said quite brightly, 'I think I might hire a car and drive up to the moors. I might even go to the coast. We used to have picnics on the beach at Bridlington. I wonder if it's changed much?'

'Don't hire a car, idiot. I'll take you.' He cut off her protests. 'I thought we had a pact? You haven't started boring me with Hollywood gossip yet, but you did promise.'

'At least you're wearing your nasty country tweeds,' she came back, 'so I suppose if you're determined to keep your side of the bargain, I'd better keep my side of it, too.'

For the rest of the meal they vied to tell each other the most abstruse stories they could find, Goldie scraping up every bit of scandal about the most outrageous stars she could think of, Lucas going into intricate detail on the joys of pheasant rearing. It was deliberately hilarious, and Goldie finished by accusing him of cheating.

'You're not supposed to be making it interesting,' she criticised.

'Nor are you.'

'You couldn't enjoy that film-set gossip,' she accused. 'It's just *too* trivial.'

'Trivial, but salacious,' he said in his most pompous voice. 'I can't wait to hear what happened to the one who took all her clothes off before she went in for the audition.'

'She got the job, of course. The only trouble was, she couldn't act anyway, so that was the last time she was contracted.' She grinned.

'Goldie,' he looked suddenly serious, 'you've never had to do anything like that, have you?'

'Honestly, Lucas, do you seriously think I would? Actually,' she went on before he could answer, 'I've been pushed into acting. It was when they were looking for a thirteen-year-old to play a bit part in one of Mother's films. I was hanging around, so it was natural they should test me. I happened to show up well on the screen test, and the rest, as they say, is history. I didn't have to do a thing. Work just kept coming in. I would never have done it if it hadn't been handed to me on a plate.'

'What would you have done?'

She laughed, but her eyes were sombre. 'I don't know. That's why I'm taking four months off to try and find out. Lucas,' she leaned earnestly across the table, 'the awful thing is, I just don't know who I am. I feel——' she shrugged helplessly '—I feel lost sometimes, as if everything that's happened has been really meant for someone else. It's like being in a dream. One day I'll wake up and find it was all a mistake.' She gave him a wide-eyed look, halving her apparent age in an instant and making him go still.

When he spoke, he said, 'Life hasn't treated

us so differently in some respects. At least you can get out of your life and start again.' He gave her a bleak smile.

Goldie wasn't surprised that Lucas had been a professional Army man, for there was something about the way he moved that suggested he would handle himself well in any situation. She watched him now as he strode to the next outcrop and stood looking out across the broad brown sweep of the moors towards the sea. He looked utterly at one with the landscape. The tough, clean outdoors look of him expressing the rock-safe and enduring person she felt he was inside.

It would be a lucky woman, she couldn't stop herself thinking, who had his shoulder to lean on for the rest of her life. She turned away. It was unlike her to be all emotional. She'd always prided herself on her independence.

Who needed men, anyway? she argued as she watched him climbing up the next bluff. They were ten a penny, weren't they? She had had no end of suitors in California. Bronzed, muscular beach boys, slim, talented screenwriters, affluent, worldly, sharp producers. There were men, men, men, wherever she went. The problem was keeping them at bay—convincing them that, no, she wasn't interested in whatever it was they were proposing.

She had often wondered who or what she was saving herself for, and now, having found out—she glanced across as Lucas called to her—she saw the irony of the situation.

'You're looking very thoughtful.' He came up beside her, handsome with wind-whipped cheeks, hair falling over his brow in a dark quiff. He wrapped his arms round her in a bear-hug, smoothing her spiky hair flat in a way he had already learned made her cross. 'Cold, isn't it? Do you want to go back?' he murmured against the side of her face.

She shivered in his arms, colder than he guessed in the silk shift, and trembling, too, to feel his arms round her—even though it seemed to be no more than a brotherly hug. She felt his face, ice-cold, press against her own.

'Roast chestnuts round a log fire would be wonderful,' he murmured. 'Unfortunately, it won't be this evening.' He stepped back, holding her with both arms pinned to her sides. 'I could ravish you here and now, Goldie. Let's go before I do something outrageous.'

'It's too cold to be outrageous,' she came back, trying to blink the water out of her eyes before he noticed it.

'You want a bet?'

She shook her head, smiling falsely and

swivelling on her heel to walk off down the track between banks of heather before he could take her up on it. He caught her up and put his arm around her waist. 'I've got all kinds of family business to attend to,' he told her, 'Not least this evening.'

'Sunday?'

'Semi-social,' he replied briefly. 'But in the time we've still got, we must meet as much as we can. I'm afraid you haven't bored me nearly as much as I hoped! I trust I've been doing well enough?'

'Not really,' she admitted, trying to match the lightness of his tone. 'But I expect if you show me this horse of yours I shall start to yawn a little.'

'I doubt that; she's beautiful,' he laughed.

She expected him to offer to show her round the stables. It would be good to ride out into the countryside together. That, at least, was something they could share, for she was a good rider and would be able to keep up with him, but he didn't say anything and there was an uncomfortable silence. When they drove back he pulled into the drive at the Woollards' and kept the engine running while she got out.

'Tomorrow,' he said, leaning towards the open passenger door, 'walk across when you've had breakfast, if you like, and I'll run you into town to pick up some warm clothes.'

He drove off then, and she saw him park the

Land Rover beneath the trees across the road. The millhouse was almost invisible from where she stood. Only the outer wall on the riverside could be seen, with a gable or two, and the curve of the drive before it vanished behind the trees. She remembered it from long ago as a dark, secret sort of place, but put that down to the fact that as children it had been forbidden to them. Now, she realised, it had been forbidden ground for another reason, for if Ravella had been having an affair with Brendan Halliwell, one of the de Maines, the last person she would have wanted on the scene was her own daughter. Sighing, Goldie made her way indoors. She felt that there was more to the brief hints about the past than met the eye, though what the secret could be, she couldn't imagine.

That evening was spent much as the previous one had been, with the addition of a little television and a visit from Hetty's son and daughter-in-law for an hour or two. Talk centred on the doings of the various members of the family, once interest in Goldie's unexpected presence was satisfied. After they had gone she went up to her room and wondered if there would be another awakening like the one on the previous night, but the clock in the hall downstairs struck twelve before she gave up on that hope.

Unable to sleep, she got up and padded across the landing to the bathroom to get herself a drink of water. Lights across the road made her pause before switching on the one in the bathroom. A car was revving up and there was the sound of laughter. Unable to help herself, she went to the window and stood on tiptoe to peer out through the unfrosted top half of the glass.

It was too dark to make anything out, but, headlamps blazing, a car came purring down the drive, followed closely by a second. Visitors, she guessed.

She got her drink in the dark and went back to bed. He was free to have guests to dinner. Family business, he had told her. It had been a girl's laugh, high and flirtatious, a little drunk. Well, why not? Lucas had his life to lead. She herself was just passing through.

It was nearly half-past ten by the time she found herself walking up the drive the next morning between dark, overreaching conifers. She rang the bell and waited. Almost at once the door flew open. 'You get up late? Or did you imagine I meant lunchtime?' He was smiling, his hair gleaming darkly in the splintered light that came in from outside, and in an open-necked checked shirt and a pair of chestnut-brown corduroys he looked more informal, but as endearing as ever.

'I thought you might be still sleeping off the effects of your business meeting last night,' she replied, somewhat stiffly.

His eyes danced. 'Would that I were!' came the cryptic response. 'It's all part and parcel of being a de Maine, there can be an awful lot of social responsibilities.'

She didn't know whether he meant he wished he was sleeping it off with whoever his guest had been, or something else, so she merely gave him a non-committal smile and went inside as he held the door. When it closed she looked round with interest. It was the sort of place she liked, but not the sort she often found herself in.

Everything was old and well-worn, with the patina of age and much loving care on it. There was a faint smell of lavender wax and the musk of wood-smoke in the air, and, she detected a minute later, freshly ground coffee, too.

'It's good timing,' he confirmed. 'I'm just making coffee, having given you up.'

He led the way into a large, comfortable kitchen while she wondered if he would have bothered to come over to find her if she hadn't made a move. There was a big pine table, well-scored with years of use, and half a dozen comfortable matching chairs with flowered cushions in russet tones to match the curtains. A black and white dog was lying in a basket with its head on its paws, and as soon as Goldie came in it leaped up and came over to her, sniffing suspiciously, and backing off, wagging its tail when Lucas murmured something.

'What's he called?' Goldie bent to pet the dog, but Lucas shook his head. 'I wouldn't do that. He's a gun dog, and not used to being treated like a pet.'

Rebuked, Goldie wandered over to the window and looked out. Damn his dog, she thought. Her high heels had made a silly tapping sound as she crossed the stone-flagged kitchen floor, and she was suddenly overwhelmed by the feeling of being out of place again. The funny thing was, she could almost forget it. It just took a stray remark from Lucas to remind her. It was as well. Obviously he never forgot for a minute that she didn't belong in his milieu.

He was putting two mugs on the table when she turned round, then, apparently thinking better of it, went back to the Welsh dresser and took down two red and white French coffee-cups with saucers. She didn't comment, even when he glanced at her to see if she'd noticed.

'I'm sorry,' he said when he brought the coffee-pot to the table and she still hadn't spoken. 'He's not used to being fondled. I'd hate you to get bitten.'

'I thought the English were supposed to be

animal lovers?' she came back, still hurt.

'Loving something doesn't mean making it lose its dignity. Sometimes you have to be cruel to be kind.' He glanced away, as if not wanting to pursue the matter, and Goldie wondered if he really did find her ignorance of his ways rather tedious, after all.

'Is this where my mother and Brendan used to meet?' she asked, looking round the cosy kitchen with a belligerent air.

'I expect so. That was a bit before my time. His studio's upstairs, more or less as it was. You can have a look, if you like.' He poured the coffee and offered her a biscuit from a tin with a picture of a cottage garden on the side. Picking up his cup and saucer, he said, 'Come on.'

She followed meekly upstairs. There were several doors leading off the landing, but he led her to one at the far end. It opened on to a large, light, north-facing studio in the eaves. An easel and several unfinished canvases lay scattered about, as if somebody had just gone out for a few minutes.

'These surely can't be Brendan's? Do you paint?'

Lucas laughed and shook his head. 'I only buy and sell. I don't do the stuff myself. This lot hasn't been used for years.' He picked up a tube of oil-paint and she saw that it was rock-hard. 'Somebody might get around to clearing out all his stuff some day. I don't know who. I'm only the lodger. It does no harm here, and until the room's needed for something more urgent it may as well stay.'

'I thought he died years ago,' Goldie said, confused.

'He did. Nine, actually.' Lucas watched her closely.

'That was after we left,' she said, more for something to say.

Lucas nodded. His expression was quite cold. 'I was fond of him. It was a bad business. I was in the Army by then, but I always felt somebody could have done something.'

'Why? What do you mean?'

'Don't you know how he died?'

She shook her head.

Lucas moved over to the window and stood looking out at the sky and the tops of the trees. 'I thought you did.'

When he turned back, he was frowning. 'Did Ravella never say anything?'

Again Goldie shook her head.

Lucas spread his hands. 'I'm sorry. Maybe we shouldn't have started on all this.'

'Tell me, Lucas. You must tell me, now. What happened?'

'He went missing. They found his body in the river two days later.'

'He slipped and drowned?'

'Not slipped. No. It was deliberate. That summer ten years ago was just too much for him. He'd been in love with your mother for years. I guess he just couldn't take any more.'

'But that was the summer you said she was involved with—oh, Lucas! Is it true?'

He shrugged. 'It was quite a summer.' He gave a short laugh. 'It wasn't her fault, for heaven's sake. But people have long memories round here. They rarely forget, and they never forgive. You're her daughter, Goldie. It's not your quarrel. But——'

'But what, Lucas?' She was puzzled and her face expressed it.

He turned away. 'But people will paint you in the same colours, of course.' He went to the door. 'Drink your coffee and let's go.' His glance skimmed over the T-shirt and tiny mini, but he didn't say anything, and when she went to walk past him to go downstairs again he stepped back so their bodies didn't touch.

CHAPTER FIVE

WHEN they went out to the Land Rover Goldie felt she had to say something. Things seemed to have deteriorated between them for no good reason, with first the trivial incident with the dog, then the shattering revelation about Brendan. Now she felt she was somehow in Lucas's debt, being given a lift so she could do some shopping.

'You don't have to take me into town, you know,' she began, standing beside the driver's door as he unlocked it.

'I know. I offered.'

'You didn't have to——'

'There's not much I do have to do. Apart from occupy the slot allotted to me. Get in.' He swung up, but when she went on standing there he didn't close the door, but looked down at her and said, 'You don't intend to go around dressed like that much longer, do you?'

'Does it really bother you?' she demanded, feeling a rush of anger at the veiled insult, but he simply burst out laughing.

'Goldie, you can wear whatever pleases you. But you'll surely get your death of cold if you

85

don't buy something warmer. Now, do you have anything better to do this morning?'

'No . . .' she began doubtfully.

'And neither have I. So get in and let's go.'

When she was sitting beside him he said, 'If it makes you feel any better, I'll probably have to have a word with my saddler to see how he's getting on with a job I gave him last week. Better?'

'Tons,' she remarked drily. It had been close enough to a genuine argument, unlike the bantering of their previous differences of opinion, for her to feel sobered by it. She thought, if we can't do the simplest thing without getting into an argument, then what hope, is there? But she already knew there was no hope anyway, so it really made little difference. She tried to remember advice she had heard at different times, like 'take one day at a time', or 'live in the present and let tomorrow take care of itself'. But still it made little difference. She wanted him now. And she was miserable now, because she knew she would never have him, neither today nor tomorrow.

The market town was busy with shoppers. Lucas managed to find a piece of wasteland on which to park the Land Rover, and then he walked her through a back alley until they came to the high street again. To Goldie's eyes there seemed to be a marked lack of boutiques. All she could see was a tiny shop with a couple of suits in the window which she wouldn't be seen dead in, and she wondered if Lucas imagined she would ever wear anything like that. She didn't say anything, waiting for him to make suggestions, as the idea that she could get something had come from him in the first place.

'You need something warm and practical for this afternoon, and something a bit smarter for——'

'This afternoon?'

'I've got to walk the estate. I do it every week. Don't you want to come with me?'

'Oh, yes,' she replied hurriedly. She didn't know what he meant, but she'd go for a short walk with him. It would make a change to be out.

'And you'll need something smarter for London,' he went on. He glanced at the two suits in the window as they slowed down, then glanced at Goldie. 'I think not,' he murmured. 'Even I would draw the line at those.'

'I don't think I'm going to get anything to suit me, Lucas. Not what you would call smart.' She gave him a sidelong glance. 'I feel I'm going to look all right in London like this.' She was conscious of the looks as they walked along, and knew that Lucas had registered them, too. 'It'll be different in a big

city like London. Here, I admit I do make
people stare. I'm sorry,' she added, wondering
why she should be apologising.

He gave a short laugh. 'I'm not—sorry, I
mean. You look fantastically sexy, that's why
they're staring. You're like a creature from
another planet.' He turned to her, and the
expression she had thought was indifference
she now saw as self-control. The expression in
his eyes revealed exactly what he was feeling,
and he was actually turned on by her!

For a second their bodies brushed and he
put out an arm, pulling her against him. 'You
seem to have some crazy idea I want to change
you,' he murmured.

'I'm only remembering what you said to me
when we first met,' she told him.

'What was that?'

'"You're not exactly my type",' she quoted.

'It's true.' He laughed. 'I'm not your type,
either, if you're honest. It doesn't mean we're
not going to respond to each other. Hell, I'd
have to be dead from the neck down to be
unmoved by you, by your . . .' Looking into
her eyes he seemed to lose the thread. 'Look,'
briskly, he stepped back, 'let's get you a pair
of jeans, a good warm sweater and a pair of
boots. You can't walk the fields in high heels.'

He led her to the saddlers, and while she
riffled among the waxed jackets and jodhpurs
and crisp rows of jeans and oiled-wool

sweaters he finished his business with the old man behind the counter, then came over to her.

'Found anything?'

She dragged out a pair of size eight jeans. 'These should fit. But I can't find any sweaters under a size thirty-six. I'll try the jeans, and one of these wool shirts. And I'll just slip a sweater on top to see if it's really too big.'

When she came out from behind the curtain that marked off a corner of the shop as a changing-room, he was standing with his hands in his pockets waiting for her. She burst into giggles when she saw his expression. 'All right, the sweater's too big.' She took it off. 'But the jeans and shirt are OK. What do you think?'

She glanced up and caught the look in his eyes. He turned away at once, a half-smile on his lips, knowing she had read what was in his mind. 'Here,' he said, pretending to be absorbed in choosing something else for her as an assistant came up. 'Try a waterproof, too.'

'I wondered when I'd finish up in one of these,' she murmured, taking it from him and slipping it on. The dark green colour suited her. She put the corduroy collar up and gazed at herself in the full-length mirror. It was a total transformation, despite her blonde hair and Californian tan. She almost looked as if she belonged.

'And a pair of boots,' he suggested. 'You'll need thick socks as well.'

Fully kitted out, she went over to him. He was over by the cash desk, writing a cheque, and when she came up he said, 'I take it you're going to keep it all on?'

'I feel like somebody playing a part. Where are the cameras?' she joked, then when she saw what he was doing she protested. He shushed her and she had to wait until her old clothes were parcelled up and they were outside the shop.

'Don't insist on paying. I shall feel insulted,' he told her, in a tone implying he would brook no objections. 'Remember, thanks to you I made quite a handsome commission on Saturday.'

'How do you mean?' she asked.

'By the strange logic of these things, the more of my clients' money I spend, the bigger amount I receive. It's to do with the percentage,' he added.

She began to laugh. 'And you said I owed you.'

'I felt you did at the time. I'm always willing to have second thoughts.' He took her by the arm. 'I'm hungry after all that. And I think you're right. We'll give the Bond Street image a miss today. You can always pick something up when we're down there.'

'Lucas, how long are you intending to stay?'

'I thought a couple of days. How long do you think you can spare?'

Her lips tightened. 'A couple of days in London?' She didn't look at him.

'How long can you spare?' he insisted again.

'I can spare all the time in the world,' she told him icily, 'but that's hardly the point.' She couldn't believe what she had heard. 'When you offered to give me a lift to town, to the airport, I thought that's what it was going to be.' She could scarcely speak for anger. 'Now I see there are to be strings. Payment. I'm sorry, Lucas, I didn't realise that was your intention——'

'Hey, wait, you've lost me.'

'Have I?' she asked, giving him a bleak look full of barely concealed disdain.

He didn't reply, but instead hurried her into the entrance of the only hotel on the high street. An old coaching inn, it still retained some of the features from its former days when mail was its main trade. Lucas sat her down beside the good log fire and ordered a couple of drinks.

'Right, let's get this straight. You think I'm trying to lure you to London so I can have my wicked way?' He laughed mirthlessly. 'Really, Goldie, you've taken part in too many films. Real life isn't like that.'

'Isn't it?'

'I don't know,' his expression hardened,

'maybe it is for you. Certainly for me it isn't. I don't seduce helpless young girls by having to promise them a couple of days on the town.' He looked so annoyed, in fact insulted by the idea, she gazed at him with a sinking feeling, knowing that it had happened again. She'd somehow misread him, drawing attention to their differences once more.

He underlined this impression when he went on, 'You might give me credit for some style. Or do you see me as some kind of amateur lecher, fumbling around in hotel bedrooms?'

'I certainly don't see you as amateur, Lucas,' she said, in clipped tones to mask her dismay.

'A professional lecher sounds even worse,' he observed. 'I suppose that's the sort of world you're used to. With people jumping in and out of bed with each other all the time with no dignity, no depth of feeling, no real emotion. And because you're so hardened to it, you don't realise that there's a different world where people love honestly and truly, faithful unto death.' His dark eyes clouded and she knew the memory of Brendan had come into his mind, so that he hardly needed to mention Ravella and how she had lived, and the example—the bad one—she had given to her daughter.

Goldie was just about to say she knew all that, and that Ravella wasn't as bad as she was painted, and nor was it her style, either, to jump in and out of bed, when her attention was diverted by a burst of laughter from a group of people coming in through the door. They came up to Lucas, surrounding him and shaking his hand and greeting him in a generally effusive way, so that all possibility of continuing such a conversation was lost.

There were three men and a young woman, all obviously old friends of Lucas. They pulled up chairs and ordered drinks, and then turned briefly to Goldie when he mentioned her name, but were all far too interested in telling Lucas about some incident or other concerning people they all, except Goldie, knew. Lucas, still disdainful of her, made little effort to invite her into the conversation, so that she sat there, feeling out of place yet again, and wondering if she should just get up and walk away.

Eventually everybody ordered sandwiches, and Goldie had to endure the tedium of conversation about people she didn't know and cared less about. In five minutes I'm going to leave, she told herself. And when five minutes elapsed she gave them all another five minutes, and when the hand on the clock over the fireplace had moved on a further quarter of an hour she calmly got to her feet and went towards the door.

He'll think I'm going to the loo, she

thought. Maybe I ought go back and say I'm leaving? But she felt too angry and disheartened, and simply wanted to get right away, as far as possible, and never see Lucas again.

The whole thing had been impossible from the first. It was one thing to say it, but quite another to have to experience it.

She went outside and stood for a minute looking up and down the high street. There seemed to be a bus-stop at one end, so she walked over to it in her new boots, feeling self-conscious until she realised that nobody was really looking at her any longer because she merged in so well with the rest of them. She scanned the bus timetable, but couldn't make any sense out of it.

'Excuse me,' she asked tentatively of a woman with a shopping basket who was standing close by, 'is there a bus to Little Skidby?'

The woman puckered her brow. 'I don't think it goes out there today.' She came over to the timetable and peered up at it. 'You could get one to the crossroads and then walk,' she suggested. 'It'll only be a couple of miles.'

Goldie nodded her thanks and set off down the street. She knew how far it was. It was at least three miles from the crossroads. But, if that was the only way of getting back, that's what she would have to do.

It wasn't until she was on the bus that she realised that she could probably have got a taxi. But by then it was too late. The bus was speeding along the country lanes with no sign that it was ever going to stop. She noticed after a minute or two that it was beginning to rain. And that, in her haste to get away, she'd left her parcel of clothes behind.

She only hoped Lucas would have the sense to bring them with him. They would meet briefly when he called with them this evening, and then they need never meet again. Or, alternatively, maybe he would be tactful enough to leave them in the porch where she would see them. That would be the stylish thing to do, she guessed. It would certainly be the least painful.

When the bus dropped her off at the crossroads she stood for a moment, shaken by the desolation of the countryside in which she found herself. Bare hedgerows stretched on either side into the distance, and fields undulated as far as the eye could see without apparent pattern.

Already the rain was starting to fall quite heavily, and as she set off to walk it slanted inside the collar of her new waxed jacket until she thought to pull it up, fastening the storm-buttons, suddenly glad of it. Her feet felt quite snug and dry in the rubber boots and, thrusting her hands deep into her pockets, she trudged on, dry despite the weather, though none the more pleased because of it.

Every step took her further from the scene of what she was beginning to see as deliberate humiliation by Lucas in front of his friends. He was ashamed of her, that went without saying, hence the deliberately sketchy introductions and subsequent ignoring of her while they all got on with their own conversations. Obviously she had done the right thing in walking out, and she wondered how long it would be before he noticed she had gone.

She went on for about a mile, with the rain coming down harder every minute. Every time a car passed she had to step on to the grass verge, and it crossed her mind to try to thumb a lift, but on reflection she thought it safer in such an isolated spot to keep on walking as if she knew where she was going.

Soon her hair was plastered to her scalp and her cheeks were beginning to sting. It was almost impossible to see where she was going without taking a hand out of her pocket every so often and rubbing the back of it across her eyes. The worse it got, the more she hated Lucas for making her run out like that. She hoped he would bring her things round so she could give him a piece of her mind. But she thought so badly of him by now, she doubted whether he would even bother to carry her things out from beneath the table they had been sitting at, let alone bring them over to the house for her.

She was trudging along in this mood when she heard a car behind her and, half turning, stepped back on to the verge to let it pass as those before had. But it slowed and she heard an irritable hooting on the horn, making her lift her head with a scowl to peer back through the rain. Her heart thudded at the familiar sight of the Land Rover skidding to a halt behind her, half on the verge and half off.

With the engine still running, Lucas sat inside, presumably expecting her to go back and get in.

Over my dead body, she thought furiously. With a jerk of her head she spun round and began walking on down the road. Another toot on the horn accompanied her, but she kept on walking with the wild idea that if she ignored him he would simply go away.

Suddenly the Land Rover was right beside her. The passenger window opened and she heard Lucas saying in a peremptory tone, 'Get in, Goldie. Hurry up, for heaven's sake! What are you playing at?'

She gave a short laugh and marched on as if he hadn't spoken. The engine revved hard then, and she saw the vehicle lurch forward, coming to a halt just in front of her. As she drew level, Lucas leaped from the driver's seat and lunged towards her.

'What the devil do you think you're doing, you stupid idiot? I could have run you over, and then what?' He shook her so violently, she nearly fell when he released her. She lifted a hand and was about to strike him when she thought better of it.

'Don't you dare touch me, you brute!' she yelled instead, all her pent-up anger exploding in a sudden volcano of rage. 'Why don't you get back to your precious friends instead of following me about the countryside? I'm sure they're far more interesting to somebody like you. I don't know how you can bear to drag yourself away from them!'

'What the hell did you walk out for, you stupid fool?' he rasped, ignoring what she'd said. 'Do you realise I've spent the last hour going into every damned shop in town asking if they'd seen you? I thought you'd been abducted—though who the hell would want to abduct you, heaven knows!' He gazed down at her with eyes full of ire. 'You look terrible, like a drowned rat. Some Hollywood starlet, I must say!' A derisive laugh was wrenched from his throat. 'If you were wearing your old clothes, you'd be soaked to the skin,' he observed with satisfaction. 'Why didn't you think before you set out?'

'It wasn't raining when I left, that's why. Do you think I'm a weather prophet? Though you, no doubt,' she drew herself up, 'as a true peasant, can probably predict the weather from the flocking of ravens.'

'From clouds, actually, though more usually I turn the radio on.' He almost smiled. 'Look, get in, Goldie. I'm getting wet, too, standing out here.'

'Should I care?' she shouted, backing away. 'I'd rather be dead than go anywhere with *you*!'

She turned and began to run down the road as fast as she could. She wanted to turn to see how he'd taken that, but dared not in case he was right behind her. In a second or two she heard the Land Rover start up again and come rattling after her.

Once more he stopped in front of her, but this time she was ready, and when he came round the side of it she ran the other way and carried on without looking back, jogging on down the lane, slipping and sliding now in the mud as she reached some trees in a little copse that straddled the road. She heard the engine start up again, but this time he merely chugged along behind her, making her feel suddenly childish to be behaving like this. It seemed as if he was always putting her in the wrong, just as he had done on that first day at the auction. Feeling humiliated, she turned and ran up to the open window, and glared in at him.

'I hate you, Lucas de Maine. You're so self-

righteous, you make me sick. You can just go
to hell!' She remembered what he had said in
the hotel and, spurred on by the injustice of it,
she added, 'You seem to think yours is the
only way to live, but let me tell you, you're
wrong. Just because you've done a bit of
travelling in the Army, you think you know
everything, but you haven't a clue about other
people. You're stuck in this narrow, feudal
little backwater like some caveman——' She
stopped. She hadn't meant to say quite that. It
might make him think she thought he was
macho. He was, but that wasn't the point.

She opened her mouth to continue, but he
cut in, saying, 'Have you quite finished?
Because, if so, I'm going to ask you once more
to get in. If you don't, I'm driving on and to
hell with you, too.'

'Good! That's the best news I've heard yet.
Get going, damn you!' She hit the side of the
Land Rover with her clenched fist, satisfied
when it made a dull, tinny rumble.

'So that's your last word, is it?' His white
face peered through the window at her.

'You bet it is, buster!' She felt she
remembered saying those particular lines in a
film, but before she could work it out he gave
a sort of snarl of anger and gunned the engine.
The Land Rover shot off through the closing
curtains of rain, and soon she was trudging
along in a silence made all the more profound

because of the shouting that had preceded it.

It was a good half-hour before she reached the village, and then she had the humiliation of walking through it in a thoroughly wet and dishevelled state, self-consciously imagining that everyone could tell what had been going on. She knew she had behaved childishly, but once started it had been impossible to stop. It was like the auction, when she had simply gone on bidding because of the roller-coaster effect.

Still, Lucas was beyond the pale. Pride would never let her bend to him now.

She had got as far as the gate, hurrying with her head down as the skies seemed to open up, when a figure loomed in her path.

'Cooled off yet?' growled a voice in her ear.

She skidded to a halt, but not before her shoulders had been taken in a firm grip, swivelling her round.

'Go away, Lucas! I'm soaked and it's all your fault!' she shouted in his face.

'Nonsense. I asked you several times to get into the Land Rover. It was entirely your decision to walk it.'

'I'm not standing here arguing. Let me go. I want to go in to get dried.' She tried to struggle out of his grasp, but he held her more firmly.

'Come back to the millhouse and have a hot bath. You'll be getting pneumonia at this rate.'

'So what?' she argued, trying to writhe out of his arms. 'A lot you care!'

'It's silly not to look after yourself. You're not a child, though heaven knows you've been acting like one this afternoon.'

'*I* have? Of all the cheek!' she yelled, face flushing with renewed rage. 'I suppose it's childish to feel bored when a lot of boring people are talking among themselves? What was I supposed to do—sit and listen like the invisible woman?' She started to beat at his chest, as he didn't seem to have any intention of releasing her, but he grabbed her by the scruff of the neck and held her at arm's length like a puppy.

'I know any trick you might think of and a hundred more,' he told her grimly, 'so save your efforts. Now, for once do as you're told.'

He started to frogmarch her across the lane.

'I've got to go in and see Hetty; she'll be worried,' she protested, digging in her heels so that her feet skidded along when he simply dragged her with him.

'No, she won't. She's gone. Both of them have. There was a note on the door and the key under a plant-pot. Her daughter's gone into labour, and they've gone over to be with her.'

'What?' She tried to stand upright long

enough to see his face to find out whether he was making it up or not, but she could tell by the way he spoke that he meant it.

'I've got the note in my pocket,' he told her when they reached his front door and he had to release her to unlock it. 'You can read it once you've had your bath.'

'If you imagine I'm going to have a bath with you skulking around——' she began, then stopped, remembering how scathing he had been before about her assumption he only wanted to seduce her.

He gave a sigh and bundled her into the house. 'Boots off on the mat, please. I don't want Mrs Turner having to clean up your muddy footprints.' He waited while she took off her boots. 'Now the jacket,' he ordered.

'You're so damned bossy!' she snarled. 'Can't you behave like a normal human being instead of some tinpot sergeant major?'

'Certainly, when I'm faced with a normal human being. You, however, are behaving exactly as I would expect a spoiled Hollywood starlet to behave. Flouncing out when you fail to become the centre of attention. Hurting yourself rather than giving in gracefully when you know you're in the wrong.'

'You smug devil!' she shouted, beside herself with anger at the cool nerve of the man. 'I've heard some distortions, but that takes the biscuit! I sat there for hours being bored out of my mind while you and your friends rattled on about damn all! Centre of attention? It was all any of you could do to acknowledge my existence. Why the hell should I sit there and listen to your drivel?'

'I'm sorry if you feel so strongly about a simple drink with friends of mine,' he told her coldly. 'We both knew from the moment we met that we had nothing in common beyond a superficial sexual attraction. I hadn't wished to bore you to quite such a degree of distraction.'

His face was expressionless. Goldie wanted to hit him to get some sort of spontaneous response, to get some sort of warmth from him, but he preserved a manner of icy indifference as he told her where the bathroom was. 'It's no good your going over to Hetty's. They left soon after we did this morning, turning off the central-heating system, not knowing when you'd be back. Here, read their note. They're going to ring here round about teatime.'

'Here? Why here?'

'Because they mistakenly assume we're in the throes of a romantic relationship, I expect.' He smiled tightly and went out, leaving her to climb upstairs in her soggy clothes and lock herself in his bathroom. She sat on the edge of the bath as it rapidly filled with hot water, and listened to her heartbeats. They were twice as fast as they ought to be. It was terrifying what anger could do. She had never hated anyone as much as she hated Lucas de Maine.

CHAPTER SIX

WHEN she came downstairs after her bath she was wearing a man's brocade dressing-gown she'd found hanging on the bathroom door. Her own clothes were too wet to put back on. She carried them in a soggy bundle and stood in the kitchen doorway, wondering where she could dry them. She couldn't escape until she had some dry clothes to put on.

Lucas looked up when he heard her and came over, taking the jeans and the checked shirt from her. 'They'll dry in front of the Aga,' he told her, giving her a piercing glance as if to judge her mood now she'd had time to cool down.

His expectation that she might be ready to back down irked her just as much as his words earlier, and she pushed past him and went to stand beside the Aga herself.

'You'd better have a tot of rum,' he said as he arranged her clothes on the bar next to her. 'But I've made a pot of coffee, too.'

I'm supposed to fall over myself with gratitude, she thought angrily. Well, I shan't! She merely nodded, her expression one of disdain, and went over to the pot on the table, pouring herself a cup then replacing the pot, even though his own cup was empty and waiting beside hers. He noticed her omission without comment, and she could almost feel him thinking how like a typical spoiled starlet. She turned back to the Aga with a tightening in her throat that made it almost impossible to swallow the hot black liquid.

'That was yes, please, to the rum, wasn't it?'

'I'm sorry,' she said in her coldest tones, 'I didn't realise I had to put in an application for it.' She didn't look at him.

'Some people don't like rum. I couldn't assume you did, without asking.'

'Why not? You assume plenty of other things.' She half turned, blushing when she saw the way he was looking at her.

'I thought I had reasonable grounds for the assumptions I'd made about you so far,' he rasped.

'Of course,' she replied sarcastically. '*Very* reasonable grounds!' She knew she was behaving badly, but he was driving her to it with his smug, supercilious clarity. Why couldn't he be wrong-footed for once? She ignored him while she drank her coffee, and when he pushed a fragile glass of dark rum towards her she sipped it rapidly, not caring if it burned her throat.

Despite all he had done for her since she came in, she was beginning to shiver. He regarded her without speaking for as long as he could, then got up suddenly with a short exclamation. He went out and came back almost immediately with a plaid rug in his hands.

'I don't damn well care if you imagine you create a more glamorous effect in that dressing-gown. Get this over you, will you?' He flung the rug at her, making her reach out automatically to catch it.

She draped it over one arm. 'All right?' she demanded.

'Not all right,' he growled. He crossed towards her. 'Damn you, you know how I mean. Like this.' Reaching out, he draped the rug over her shoulders, then, gripping it on either side, he held her trapped for a moment, looking down at her with a strange expression on his face before slowly beginning to pull her in towards him. 'You're really asking for it, darling. You really are . . .' He seemed to tower over her, keeping her trapped, making shudders of a different kind scud over her as she saw what was in his mind.

'I don't know what you mean——' she began in her most frigid tones, trying to step back and failing. They swayed together and he tightened the rug around her again, so that their bodies were touching.

'I mean when you come down hot from a bath with all that pink nudity showing in the opening of your gown, flashing your naked thighs at me——' His voice had grown husky and he lowered his head a little. 'I mean, that's when you're really asking for it.' Again his head lowered, his mouth curving in the beginnings of a smile. 'Am I right?' he whispered as he lowered his lips to hers.

For a moment she resisted, all his accusations ringing in her ears, but then the demanding mastery of his touch triumphed and she sank against him, opening her lips to the exploring tongue, submitting with a soft sigh to the movement of his hands over her naked skin beneath the stiff brocade. Reaching up helplessly, she slid her arms round his neck, arching against the hard muscles moulding themselves against her slender form, allowing him to take possession of her with an impulsive, instinctual reaction that was wholly new.

His tongue probed victoriously into her mouth, establishing his mastery, melting all thoughts of resistance while his body crushed against hers, his hands moving rhythmically over her small body, bending it to his will. The brocade dressing-gown had slipped off one shoulder, and she shuddered with pleasure as his lips explored the hollows at the base of her neck, circling over the nakedness revealed beneath. With a harsh exclamation he pulled the gown right open, trailing sensual fingers from the tips of her breasts down over her tautening stomach to the intimate V of her legs.

At once she heard an inner warning, but his touch was so masterful that her doubts were overcome by the clamouring voices of desire. 'Lucas!' she whispered, as if by uttering his name she could tell him everything that was in her heart. 'Oh, Lucas . . .'

A sudden hammering at the door shattered the silence, making Lucas jerk his head up with a muffled curse. 'Who the hell . . .?' The sound came again, even more insistently. 'I'll have to go,' he groaned. 'They'll have seen the Land Rover in the drive. They'll know I'm here.'

Despite the hammering at the door, he slid his hands slowly and sensually back over her naked body till he held her face between them, then he bent to give her one last hot kiss on the lips before pulling the rug tightly around her, as if protecting a precious object from view. 'I won't be long.'

He swivelled out and she heard voices at the front door. Wonderingly, she touched her burning lips, feeling even now the afterglow of his touch on her silky skin, and marvelling at the ease with which he had overcome her resistance. But the respite gave her a chance to come back to earth, and she was shocked to think how easily she had submitted. Events were leading in only one direction, and but for the interruption she would probably be in his bed by now. He had taken complete possession of her mind and body. It could only confirm the impression he already had of her.

Angrily she fumbled for the belt of the dressing-gown and tied it in a tight knot, then, obeying his orders now it was too late, pulled the tartan rug over her shoulders, concealing every scrap of tan flesh from view. She went to sit in one of the wooden armchairs by the kitchen table, every nerve alert for the battle of wills that would start the minute he came back.

There was a sound of the front door slamming and footsteps over the wooden floor. The kitchen door swung open.

'I have to go out. Keep yourself warm. And if I'm not back soon, get yourself something to eat.' He indicated the fridge. 'Plenty in there. But look around. OK?'

'Go out?' she demanded, but he had already gone back into the hall. She heard him banging about in one of the cupboards, and when he returned he had on his waterproof jacket and a gun over one arm.

'Lucas!' she exclaimed.

He grinned at her surprise. 'You're in the country now, darling. There's a dog worrying our sheep up at Waudby Rig. Let's hope I won't be long.' With that he came over to her, and before she could move he bent down and, with the gun crooked over one arm, dragged her face up to his with the other and gave her a searing kiss on the lips. Her whole body screamed out for him, despite her intentions to resist, and his answered hers before he tore himself away with a sudden drawn expression on his face and a growl of regret.

He left without saying anything.

After the door closed behind him, Goldie put her head in her hands. It wasn't safe to stay. She couldn't handle this. He was too much. Everything he had said recently showed that she would only be a quick fling as far as he was concerned. And she wanted more than that. It would be all or nothing for her.

When she was sure he had gone, she got up quickly and took off the rug and the dressing-gown, going over to the Aga and taking down her still damp clothes and slipping into them with a shudder of displeasure. Folding up the things he had lent her, she went into the hall and donned her waterproof and boots. There was no sign of the parcel with her old clothes in it, and she wondered if he had left it behind after all. Still, it could wait. The important thing was to get away before he came back.

It was freezing cold at Hetty's, and she kept

her coat on while she searched around for the central-heating switch. It was nowhere to be found and, after pressing various switches in an airing cupboard, she finally gave up; gingerly removing her coat and boots, she went upstairs and tucked herself into bed. The sheets were desperately cold and she shivered for an hour or two, trying out all the remedies from thinking warm to breathing into her socks to improve matters. Nothing worked. Soon her teeth began to chatter and she decided to go downstairs in a minute and make a cup of tea.

She must have dozed off then, for when she woke up it was twilight and the rain seemed to have stopped at last. Her limbs felt stiff from lying with her knees bunched up in an effort to hug some warmth back into herself. But it wasn't that that had aroused her. Turning her head slightly, she gave a little gasp.

'Oh, it's you!' she exclaimed ungraciously, sitting up at once. 'How did you get in?'

'I have a spare key.'

'One of the rights of the lord of the manor?' she jibed, determined to start off by showing her resistance straight away.

'Hardly.' He smiled. 'When they're away I look after their dogs and generally keep an eye on things.'

'That's why the dogs didn't bark when you were prowling round here the other night,' she observed.

'Dogs like me, anyway. Apart from the one I've just shot. They know I won't stand for any nonsense,' he told her.

She shivered. 'You're barbaric.'

'Someone's got to protect the sheep.'

She turned her head. 'I'm sorry for what happened over at the millhouse. It must have given you the wrong impression. I can't imagine what came over me. I don't usually lose control like that.'

'No?' Plainly he didn't believe her.

'No!' she retorted, dragging the duvet right round her. 'After what you'd said, it was the last thing I expected. You took me completely by surprise.'

'If only I had.'

'What?' she asked puzzled.

He leaned forward and said huskily, 'Taken you. Any way. Every way. It's what we both wanted.'

She blushed violently, moving away and coming up abruptly against the wall on the other side of the single bed. She drew her knees up as some sort of protection. He observed the movement with a detached smile. 'Don't worry, Goldie. The heat of the moment has passed. Neither of us wants to lose control like that again.'

'If you're going to suggest another pact like the one where you promised to bore me to death——' She stopped, unsure how to go on.

'I think the time for games is over, don't you?' he cut in. His voice had a hollow sound, and in the half-dark his eyes were only two black pits, their expression indecipherable.

Goldie's teeth were chattering again and she couldn't think of any reply. She watched as he got up from the side of the bed and went to sit at a safe distance on the window-sill. 'Why did you come back here?' he asked. 'It's much warmer over at the millhouse.'

'I thought it would be safer here,' she muttered. 'I didn't realise you had a key.'

'Well, you're safe anywhere with me. Just don't come down half-naked flashing your lovely limbs at me and expecting me to behave like a stone, that's all.'

What now? thought Goldie, tracing the pattern on the duvet. She started to sneeze.

'Come on. Get up.' He came back towards the bed, then stopped. 'Have you got anything on under there?'

She nodded, whereupon he pulled back the duvet, revealing that she was still fully clothed. He put out a hand and she flinched back, but instead he merely fingered the edge of her blouse. 'It's still damp, you idiot. Come on. Let's get you into something dry.'

Annoyed by what seemed his genuine concern, she said waspishly, 'I suppose you'd hate to feel you had my flu on your conscience?'

He nodded grimly. 'If that's how you want to see it, yes. Now come along.'

Secretly relieved to find herself back in the warmth again, she snuggled down inside the rug beside the Aga with a mug of hot cocoa cupped in her hands. He had given her a flannelette shirt of his own, and one of his big baggy sweaters to wear over it, and when she stood up it came down to her knees. But it was warm, and she began to feel a little drowsy, vaguely aware that there might have been rum in the cocoa.

He was sitting at the table now, with a newspaper spread over it and various bits and pieces of oiled rag scattered around, cleaning his gun with an intent look on his face and no obvious inclination to engage her in conversation. A clock ticked on the pine dresser and at six o'clock he switched on a radio and listened to the news. It was very peaceful. An oasis of tranquillity, she thought with a wry, inward smile. A pleasant break from the hectic life of a film star. She sighed. Other people's lives always seemed so attractive. It was a case of the grass being greener, she supposed. Many people would give their eye-teeth to have her job.

* * *

She must have slept there in the chair, for it was nearly ten o'clock when a hand on her shoulder shook her awake. Her nose felt stuffy and her eyes were sore, and when she tried to speak her voice came out in a throaty whisper that should have been seductive, but on Lucas it seemed to have no effect whatsoever.

'You'd better sleep in the spare room,' he told her briskly, clattering around once he saw she was awake. He gave her a sardonic glance. 'Don't worry,' he said before she could reply, 'I know how your mind works by now. There's a key on the inside—and I don't have a duplicate.'

He went out and she could only glower silently after him.

On reflection, she supposed it made sense to stay. At least it was warm, and she was painfully conscious of her bunged-up nose, presaging a cold. When he came back in to tell her the bed was ready he gave her a penetrating stare. 'Are you all right? You look flushed.'

'I'm fine,' she lied, not wanting to be made to feel any more grateful than she was supposed to.

'Early start tomorrow,' he said. 'Have you forgotten you're leaving?' He said it with a certain satisfaction, she thought miserably. But she gave a gasp. 'I had forgotten, sort of.' Then she followed it up with a groan. 'Oh, no! I totally forgot—I had to ring the airport today to see if I could get a flight.'

He surprised her then by saying, 'You can hardly leave without saying goodbye to Hetty and Sam.'

'Can't I?' Her eyes widened. She hadn't looked at it like that.

She stretched luxuriously in the comfortable bed and slowly opened her eyes. The rum must have worked like magic, for she felt gloriously rested and it was the best night's sleep she could remember. Birds were chirruping outside the window, and sunlight was already streaming in between the curtains. She lay there for a few moments, revelling in sheer comfort until she heard something like a vacuum cleaner on the stairs. Puzzled, she sat up. Surely Lucas wasn't up and about doing housework before driving all the way to London, was he?

She reached for her watch, then peered at it in astonishment. It said half-past eleven. She shook it and held it to her ear. But it still said the same time. Without thinking, she dashed out of bed and went to the door, flinging it open and calling, 'Lucas! Lucas! It's half-past eleven. I thought we were——' Then she froze.

Half-way up the stairs on her hands and knees was a woman in a green overall wielding the nozzle of a cleaner. She looked up as

Goldie appeared, and her reddening face took in the slim form of the nearly naked girl standing in the bedroom door. Goldie tried to pull Lucas's old shirt together at the front, but the damage had been done. To make matters worse, Lucas himself chose that moment to come bounding up the stairs two at a time. He froze to a halt half-way up, his reaction being much like that of his char.

Goldie wasn't quite sure what all the fuss was about. But she knew she had managed to create some kind of an incident.

'This is Miss Eastwood, Mrs Turner. She wasn't feeling too well last night——' Lucas put out a hand as if making a formal introduction, but Mrs Turner rose heavily to her feet.

'*Really*, Mr de Maine!' She looked once in Goldie's general direction, then turned, switching off the vacuum cleaner as she did so. 'I'll finish up here tomorrow, when it's more convenient,' she said in a decisive voice. Without another word she swept downstairs, and Goldie could hear the crackle of her overall, the sounds of departure concluded by the abrupt slamming of the front door.

'What the blazes do you think you're doing, wandering around stark naked, offending all and sundry?' Lucas demanded, following her as she retreated into the bedroom and slamming the door behind them both with a menacing thud. Anger was blazing from his eyes as he towered over her.

'My naked body has never offended anyone before!' she spat. 'What's with all this prudery? Haven't they seen flesh round here before?' She threw back her head in a derisive laugh.

'I'm not offended, far from it,' he cut in swiftly. 'But Mrs Turner was. She's an old-fashioned country woman. You can't expect her to ignore it when you suddenly appear looking like—like some Page Three . . .' His lips tightened. 'She can't be expected to understand.'

'Then you should employ somebody who does understand!' she snarled.

'I don't have any choice in the matter,' he came back. 'She's been with the family for years.'

'It seems to me you don't have any choice in one single thing!' she mocked.

He looked as if she had hit him. There was an unexpected silence, and she wondered what he was going to say next. He surprised her by curving his lips in a full smile, looking so suddenly, devilishly, heart-wrenchingly handsome that just seeing him made her stomach lurch with desire. She pivoted away with a toss of her head.

'You're probably right,' he told her, a new note in his voice. 'So what about helping me change things and really giving everybody something to talk about?' He came up behind her. 'Do you think you could live with it?'

'I'm not going to have to.' She moved away, pretending to rummage around for some clean clothes to put on.

'I wouldn't be too sure about that.'

She ignored the cryptic undertone, more worried by the note of desire that had come into his voice, knowing it spelled danger, and said briskly, 'It's quite ridiculous—all this fuss. Heavens, it's nothing. People walk around practically naked even in the streets on the coast.' Then she had a sudden thought. It stunned her for a moment, and, lifting her head, she asked slowly, 'Lucas, were you hoping to keep our relationship a complete secret?'

She paused, searching his face for a clue. 'You were, weren't you? You're ashamed of being seen with me!'

Suddenly it all began to make sense—the way he hadn't invited her to dinner with him two nights in succession, the way he had avoided taking her near the stables when she'd given him a perfect opening, and, of course, yesterday . . . 'You're ashamed to be seen to have anything to do with me,' she stated in a flat voice. 'That's why you were so offhand in the hotel. You're just an old-fashioned snob.

You couldn't bear to let your friends know we were—well,' she hesitated, searching for the right word, 'we were involved with each other.'

She tossed back her head and gave a scornful laugh, feeling that her heart would break. 'Well, I guess I've really put the cat among the pigeons—Ravella Eastwood's starlet daughter appearing naked in front of the char!'

'You take after your mother, Goldie. I shouldn't have expected anything less.' He spoke without expression. 'It's a quaint joke to you, but they'll talk about this for years. Building it into something it's not.' He shrugged, his expression grim and somehow forbidding, and she remembered the way he'd looked with the gun crooked determinedly over one arm as he had gone out to shoot the wild dog yesterday. Despite his comparative youth, he was not a man to be trifled with. She held her breath.

He went to the door and stopped when he reached it, one hand on the catch. 'May as well be hung for a sheep as a lamb, don't you think?'

She looked puzzled, letting her breath out slowly, wondering just what sort of retribution—for his whole manner spelled revenge—was in his mind.

'Come on. Get dressed. We'll go and have

lunch in the village pub, and you can be as outrageous as you like. I'll show you whether I'm a snob or not.'

'But I thought we were supposed to be going to London—I thought you had to be at a sale?'

'I couldn't wake you at six o'clock, you were sleeping like a baby,' he told her. 'And there's no way I can get down there now. It doesn't matter,' he went on, 'I'll simply ring in my bids.' He glanced at his watch. 'The Coach and Horses will be open by the time you're ready. We'll lunch there. If it's cats among pigeons you want, that's where you'll find the pigeons.'

Mystified, Goldie watched him go out. Despite the urbane manner he had adopted, she felt his new attitude boded no good for herself.

CHAPTER SEVEN

LUCAS slid Goldie's coat off her shoulders, lingering, she thought, rather too long, as if unveiling a particularly costly monument. She turned round to glare at him, but he was already acknowledging one or two greetings from some of the other diners. The Coach and Horses possessed a small and, as she now saw, exclusive restaurant overlooking the river, and the clientele were quite different from the jolly crowd of the previous Saturday night. Mainly elderly, and extremely well-dressed in a cool county sort of way, the rise and fall of their conversation could only be described as discreet.

A waiter in a white jacket and bow-tie appeared beside Goldie, dealing with her coat and pulling out her chair for her with a little flourish. He greeted Lucas by name, and the way he spoke told her as clearly as if it had been printed above their heads that Lucas de Maine was somebody special.

Goldie slipped into a chair and hid her knees under the table-cloth. Already covert glances had been cast their way. Lucas noticed, too, for he was smiling in a kind of grim, basilisk

sort of way that made Goldie shiver. She felt
like a lamb to the slaughter. But what could
happen, anyway? They didn't still burn
witches at the stake, did they? In the heavy,
genteel ambience, she was beginning to feel as
if she were guilty of gross indecency. And all
for being young and wearing a silk mini-dress!
She scowled across at Lucas.

'I hope you're getting the reaction you
wanted?'

'You certainly are—getting a reaction,' he
murmured, flicking open the menu.

She let him order, not caring what she ate,
knowing it would probably be excellent
whatever it was. He ordered wine, and when it
came she knew that was the best, too.

'I shouldn't grumble about being lunched
like this,' she began when the waiter had left
them, 'but I can't see what's so dreadful about
being seen with me. Anyone would think I had
two heads.'

'So far,' he told her, 'I've protected you,
but as you insist otherwise, you may as well
take your chance like anybody else.'

She hadn't thought of his reluctance to be
seen with her as protecting her. It gave her
something to think about.

The meal was beginning to pass smoothly
and pleasantly. Goldie was just settling back,
beginning to enjoy herself, when a couple at
the table on the other side of the room got up

to leave. They came over to Lucas.

'Darling, it's not often you're seen in here at lunchtime,' gushed a tall woman in an impeccably tailored suit.

'Things a bit slack just now?' her companion greeted Lucas with an affable smile.

'I'm supposed to be at Sotheby's, but I missed the off,' replied Lucas charmingly, rising to his feet and kissing the man's wife, or what Goldie assumed was his wife, on the cheek, and shaking the man by the hand at the same time. He resumed his place and said to the woman, 'Meet Goldie Eastwood, Rosie. Goldie, this is Rosemary Lancaster,' and when Goldie proffered a hand and the woman pretended she hadn't seen it he added, 'and her better half, Wilf Lancaster of Willow Place.'

This time she didn't offer her hand, but Wilf reached for it, anyway, pumping it up and down for so long that she wondered if he was ever going to let go.

'All set for the weekend?' asked Lucas pleasantly as the two lingered a moment.

'I've got an excellent firm of caterers over from Leeds, Lucas,' Rosemary told him. 'It's all safely in their hands.'

'I was going to ring you to ask if you minded if I brought Goldie along, as she's in the district for a few days.'

He was obviously asking for form's sake,

but Rosemary Lancaster adopted an exaggerated look of regret. 'My dear, I'm most terribly sorry.' She scarcely looked at Goldie. 'I'm afraid all the numbers are fixed now. I would if I could, but it's going to be impossible to squeeze in another one. Next time, perhaps?' Now she did look at Goldie, her smile not quite reaching her cold blue eyes. 'You'll be Ravella's daughter. I'd heard you were in the district. But I didn't realise you knew Lucas.' She took her husband by the arm. 'See you at sevenish, Lucas, darling.' And then she swept out.

'You knew she'd be here, and you knew what would happen, didn't you?' Goldie accused when they were alone again. 'But you don't have to apologise,' she added sweetly. 'I wouldn't want to go anywhere where she was the hostess.'

'It's a drinks do before the Hunt Ball on Friday,' he told her. 'I'm on the hunt committee, so I can get you in there without any problem. I'm really sorry about Rosemary, but, yes, I knew what to expect. She's so predictable.'

'And I'm to expect more of the same if I'm seen with you, I suppose?'

'If you put yourself in their way, yes, you can expect a reaction. But, please, feel free to do any damned thing you want,' he said, ironically misquoting her.

'What do you want?' she asked, her mind going still.

'I'd like you beside me. From start to finish. And don't bother about Rosemary's do, I'm giving it a miss.'

'I guess I'll risk it, then,' she told him seriously. 'So long as you want me there.'

It was a small cloud over what had turned out to be a surprisingly pleasant meal. Goldie tried not to let it bother her as they made their way back to the millhouse.

'I'm going to be on the phone for most of the afternoon,' he told her. 'You can stick around and keep me supplied with hot black coffee, if you like. Or,' he shrugged and gave a smile, 'if you've anything else you'd rather do . . . go ahead.' He hesitated. 'You do know you can stay here until Hetty and Sam come back, don't you? No strings.'

'Coffee. Hot and black. Right. And Lucas,' she bit her lip, 'thanks. It probably sounds silly, but I didn't much like the idea of staying in that big old house all alone. And, Lucas,' she made a little shrug of regret, 'I'm sorry about Mrs Turner. I didn't mean to upset her.'

His reply was a smile that was almost tender, making her want to touch him, and if she hadn't known better she would have suspected he really felt a little something for her—beyond the merely physical he had admitted to—but she knew it couldn't be. He was only being moderately nice to her just now so he could stick two fingers up at the gentry.

The afternoon was exciting for two reasons, she was thinking as she stood later at the bow-window, looking out over the garden where she could see the sun sinking slowly behind a distant wood. It was exciting because Lucas was doing some very nerve-racking bidding over the phone, dealing, she couldn't help hearing, in thousands, tens of thousands in one instance, and the sums involved made even her gulp.

And the second reason, if she turned round now, was blatantly obvious.

He was lying sprawled full length on an enormous buttoned sofa in the middle of the sitting-room. Books and references were open all around him, and scraps of paper on which he had been doing his sums were scattered all over the floor. His shirt-sleeves were rolled up, and the neck was unfastened to reveal a deeply tanned torso. His hair, usually gleamingly immaculate, was rumpled like that of a little boy in the middle of a difficult stretch of homework. There was even a spare pencil stuck endearingly behind one ear. His concentration was ferocious. Even when she brought him a cup of coffee and slid down beside him, he barely lifted his glance. He was tuned in to what was happening in the saleroom down in London. Every so often she would hear the assistant at the other end murmur the state of the bidding from the floor. When he'd clinched that particular bid, he put his hand over the receiver and gave a war whoop.

'Good price?' she asked.

'So-so. But I got it. That's the main thing.' He looked at her. 'I hate doing it like this. Impossible to tell who you're up against. It's like driving blind.' He drank the rest of his coffee and pulled a face. 'Any chance of a hot one? I've one more bid on the books.' He consulted a piece of paper and began to speak into the receiver again.

She stood up, gazing long and lovingly at him. Like this, he was too easy to love. He was like a big cuddly bear.

He looked up again and caught her glance. Still talking into the receiver, he reached out a hand, pulling her down beside him without interrupting the flow of his conversation with the man at the other end.

Her silk dress rode up as he pulled her down, and his hand slid under the hem, then suddenly he was dragging her roughly against him, the telephone crushed between them. He began to move his hands rhythmically over her thighs, his dark head buried in the side of her neck, where she felt his tongue probing with a delicious caress, making her slither against him until she couldn't tell who was who. The phone tweeted and Lucas gave a small groan, pressing his lips several times against her own in a series of short, punctuating kisses that told her he was going to stop, but didn't want to.

He managed to drag the receiver to his ear without actually releasing her, and their two faces pressed against it while he tried to listen in.

'Five,' he muttered into the mouthpiece when there was a lull, and, giving a rapid glance over his left elbow at the piece of paper he had marked out for the next bid, he added, 'Go to seven.'

There was a prolonged period when he didn't appear to have to say anything into the phone, and instead spent the few minutes available kissing Goldie thoroughly until she wanted to moan aloud with the agony of knowing he would have to stop again. He was beginning to breath heavily, and she gave a giggle when he put his lips near the receiver, imagining what the man on the other end might be thinking.

'You're outrageous, Goldie Eastwood, utterly outrageous,' he muttered. There was a voice at the other end, and Lucas replied normally enough, 'Have you reached seven yet? Then go on to eight and a half, then stop.'

'*I'm* outrageous?' she protested when he put the phone on the cushions between them. 'That's the pot calling the kettle black. I thought I was supposed to be seeing to the coffee when you dragged me down here?'

'You can see to me instead,' he said roughly, dragging her down even further so that she was lying under him. She felt her eyelids close with a heavenly feeling of helplessness as his body crushed down on hers. It was the most wonderful feeling, and she wrapped her arms tightly round his neck, trying to bring his lips down over her own again.

'Slow down, you wicked wench, I've got to clinch this last bid.' He reached out for the phone and wedged it between them so he could listen in without moving. Then he allowed his hands to roam exploratively over her slim body in its almost nothing little tube of white silk.

'Don't they teach you how to say no in Hollywood?' he teased, bringing his head down between her breasts.

'Don't bet on it. I've spent my life saying no until now,' she told him, laughing softly because it was true, and now she wanted to say yes for the very first time.

He jerked his head up, dull shock registering in the depths of his eyes, and was about to say something when the voice on the other end of the line broke into an excited stream of talk. Lucas grabbed the receiver and pressed it to his ear. 'All right and nine,' he said. His eyes were seeing something far away, the scene in the saleroom perhaps, and while he was engrossed Goldie managed to roll away from him and straighten out her dress. One of his hands groped around for her, but she avoided it and stood up.

'Yes, and nine-seven-five,' he was saying when she went out. He didn't look up.

She sat for a long time at the kitchen-table with her head in her hands, only bringing herself round to putting on the kettle after a full five minutes had elapsed. She was thanking the man at Sotheby's, whoever he was. She was thanking her lucky stars. She was thanking providence. But none of it eased the knife-wound in her heart.

She got up and poured the boiling water over the coffee grounds, watching it filter into the clear jug underneath. That look, that quick jerk of the head, had been all the eloquence he needed to tell her that up to that point in their so-called relationship he still thought of her as just another experienced little starlet with a sex-obsessed mind. Heavens, he had said as much already. Why had she thought he didn't mean it? This was the second time she'd got herself almost to the point of no return and something had come along and saved her. But this time she had changed things because she had told him something he didn't know.

When he came in his expression gave nothing away. Not whether he understood what she had told him, nor whether it made any difference. She waited, tensing as he moved close. 'That fresh coffee?' he asked, avoiding her glance.

She nodded, reaching for the pot and snatching her hand back as it collided with his.

He pulled out a chair and sat down, slumping suddenly as if all the energy had been pumped out of him. 'Quite an afternoon,' he said. Now he did look at her, searching her face with his bark-brown eyes as if requiring some comment.

'Did you get all you wanted?' she asked, meaning the pictures.

'Not all, no,' he replied.

She remembered their first meeting, when he had told Violet he always got what he wanted. Now it took on a suggestive double-meaning and she blushed.

'I suppose this is the sort of game-playing you go in for on your film sets,' he muttered. He ran two hands through the short dark hair. 'Does it make you feel good to know you've got me on the wrong foot?'

'I have?' She gazed uncomprehendingly into

his eyes.

'You can hardly imagine I was pretending in there,' he snarled, scarcely raising his voice and gesturing towards the sitting-room. 'I suppose it gives you some kind of power-kick to be able to turn men on, and, when they're nice and ready to do anything for you, turn round and kick them in the gut.' His face twisted and he suddenly lunged across the table and trapped her hand on top of it with his own. 'Satisfied, then? Is this one more to notch up? What's the prize? Tease of the year? Do they have a special awards ceremony? I wouldn't put it past you.'

'You made the running, Lucas. It's not fair to put the blame on me.' She wanted to tell him how he made her feel, and that it was as painful for her to learn that there was no way forward, but instead she said, 'I'm not going to be your hors d'oeuvre between bids. Why should I be?'

He gave a harsh laugh. 'That's a good one. If I were going to make a meal of you, Goldie, it would be more than hors d'oeuvre!' He released her hand and, even though his grip had left a red mark, she longed to feel him touch her again.

She got up. 'I suppose I'd better go.'

'Go? Where?' He raised his dark head, eyes glittering at yet more provocation.

'Obviously I can't stay here with you!' she

exploded.

'Don't you trust me?' he asked, heavily sarcastic.

'Hardly,' she riposted, matching his tone.

'You can't go and sit in that empty old house by yourself. Don't be ridiculous.'

'What the hell's it got to do with you?' she shouted.

'Because,' he explained levelly, 'I'm responsible for you. I've taken over from Hetty and Sam. So sit down and try to relax.'

'Might as well ask me to relax in a cage full of underfed lions,' she muttered, pulling out a chair with an ill grace.

'I'm underfed as well, am I?'

'You should know.' She glowered at him and wondered if she ought to risk leaving. But he would probably only come across and try to fetch her back.

'Why are you scowling like a ten-year-old?' he demanded.

'Because I don't like to think of you as my chaperon,' she retorted.

'Well, you need have no fears about my trying to get you into bed,' he told her bluntly. 'I should have gone on first impressions——'

'Even though they were wildly inaccurate?' she demanded.

'You're seriously sticking to this line about being a virgin?' he asked, disbelief written all over his face.

She tossed her head and didn't even bother to answer.

'Goldie,' his voice was soft, 'you don't have to say a thing like that. I take your point about hors d'oeuvre. It wasn't the time or the place. Couldn't you have just said you'd prefer a little more attention? I didn't mean to insult you . . .' He spread his hands. 'You simply looked so irresistible standing there in your little shift with that angelic face——' He stopped and his lip curled. 'Forget it. Let's spend a nice quiet evening in front of the television. And maybe later the Woollards will call and let us know how they're getting on. You never know your luck, they might even come back tonight.' Before she could agree or disagree, he went on, 'By rights we should be celebrating with champagne. I made a nice profit this afternoon.' He raised an eyebrow. 'Or would you see champagne as part of some devilish trick to get you into bed?'

'Now who's obsessed?' she returned, lifting her chin.

'*Touché.*' He smiled, and for the first time since coming off the phone there was genuine humour in his eyes.

CHAPTER EIGHT

THERE was rather grim news from the Woollards when their phone call finally came through. Their daughter was in hospital, said the son-in-law who made the call for them. Some minor complication had set in, and she was being kept in until the baby was born some time in the next few days. 'Sam and Hetty are helping me with the youngsters,' he told Lucas. 'Is everything all right at the house?'

'No problem,' Lucas told him. 'Tell Sam not to worry about the dogs.' When he rang off, Lucas shrugged. 'It looks as if you'll be staying a few days more.'

Goldie counted the bubbles in the glass of champagne he had insisted on opening to celebrate the victories of the afternoon, and wondered what to say.

The evening had so far been fraught with danger, for though she knew that if Lucas said he wasn't going to seduce her he meant it, every little look and gesture made her fall more deeply in love with him and yearn more desperately for him to change his mind.

When they weren't fighting like this evening he was perfect, funny and informative, and thoughtful of all her needs. She tried to make herself think of him as a country clod, but couldn't because it just wasn't true, and she cursed the superficial differences that seemed to conceal a true kinship beneath.

How could she say all this, though? Lucas had obviously stuck his neck out by making their liaison public. She couldn't expect more from him. He belonged to the de Maine dynasty. To Burgh Hall. To this little pocket of old England where she was the outcast.

'I think,' she said at last, 'I might hire a car and look up a few old friends . . . I'd quite like to stay in York,' she went on, building up the picture as she spoke. 'It's so long since I've had time just to potter around.' He didn't say anything. 'I'd really like to do some sightseeing,' she went on, and then, in case he offered to accompany her, she added, 'It'll be good to be alone for a few days. There were times on that film set when I thought I'd do anything to get away from people.'

He had accepted her plans without argument, and now, having survived a further night at millhouse, she had done exactly what she had

set out to do: hired a car, booked
into a small hotel in the city centre,
visited one or two friends, and now stood
beneath the great east window in York
Minster, trying not to wish Lucas was standing
beside her.

Later she went for a brisk walk on the walls,
trying to avoid the swarms of American
tourists, and stopping off for a pot of coffee
and some cinnamon toast in the back room of
Taylor's when she'd had enough of
sightseeing. The coffee-house was just as she
remembered, which wasn't surprising as it had
stood on this same spot for the last two
hundred years. It was all vaguely reassuring,
suggesting that love, too, could last, though
what other evidence there was she couldn't
imagine. Ravella hadn't made love seem
anything but ephemeral.

She bought some flower-sprigged dresses in
Laura Ashley, quite out of her usual style, but
somehow right for the temporary life she was
living in the country, and she matched them
with a pair of pale blue velvet slippers and
some woolly cardigans. Her best buy was a
long evening dress in palest pink, for it seemed
that the invitation to the Hunt Ball was still
on. Lucas rang her every evening before dinner
to remind her.

Eventually she ran out of the need to be alone,

and decided she would have to face up to seeing Lucas again and prepare herself for the run-up to their last goodbye. It was the ball that very evening, and, gritting her teeth, she drove carefully back over the wolds towards the particular fold in the hills containing the ancestral home of the de Maines—and more especially that of Lucas de Maine.

Lucas himself was just walking down the drive as if he was going somewhere when she swung in through the gate. Although she had warned him she would be arriving some time in the late afternoon, he still looked surprised, as if he hadn't really expected her at all. He came quickly towards the car and held the door. She was wearing one of the flower-sprigged dresses, and bunched the folds of the full skirt in one hand as she climbed out.

'You look sensational,' he murmured, reaching forward and kissing her conventionally on the cheek. 'What a change of image,' he added, taking in the short velvet jacket with the frog fastening and the pale stockings and neat patent shoes. 'You look so different,' he went on hurriedly as if he had to keep on talking. 'Are you sure you're not about to play a part in some film about honest country folk—a sort of saga of England between the wars? If you'd stayed in York any longer, no doubt you'd be arriving in medieval gear.'

She felt vaguely put out at this reaction, having secretly hoped that he would have been so knocked out by her appearance, he would have swept her into his arms at once. Instead he was unloading her bags from the car and striding on into the house as if there were a train to catch.

He, too, looked different, she noted. Gone were the baggy old corduroys and the fawn sweater with the brown leather patches. Instead he had on a pale grey suede bomber jacket she hadn't seen before, and a pair of matching light-coloured jeans. All very expensive-looking, but casual, too, like some fashionable pop star. It was a style that suited him because he had the tough physique to carry it off.

'Were you going somewhere?' she asked when she caught up with him.

'I just thought I'd have a stroll to the end of the drive,' he said, offhandedly. 'Been inside most of the day.' He avoided her glance and went through into the sitting-room. 'Want a drink?' he called back.

Expecting coffee or tea, she was surprised when he thrust a large gin and tonic into her hand. 'Here's to——' he paused, glass half-raised '—to film actresses everywhere.' He grinned.

'And farmers,' she added, 'and possibly some picture dealers, too.' They both laughed, and Goldie drank rather more than she'd intended as she tried to cover her confusion, but by then Lucas had gone back to the drinks cabinet and was fiddling around with the ice.

She took the opportunity to glance round. Everything looked slightly different. Tidier, perhaps. There were early daffodils in a brass bowl by the window, and the log fire was blazing cheerfully in the large open grate.

'It's lovely to be back,' she said before she could stop herself.

'Lovely to have you back.' He turned round and gave her a wide smile, making the commonplace rejoinder seem somehow significant. Goldie's heart leapt. Then she remembered the future.

'I've booked a flight back on the tenth,' she told him, going over to the fire and gazing into the leaping flames as if seeking inspiration. 'I decided after the last film I needed to have a break and really sort out my priorities. I thought I'd take off to the mountains, do some meditation, live simply, that sort of thing.'

'Won't you miss your friends?'

'I'll find out when I get there.' She tried to laugh, but it came out as a sort of grunt and she turned it quickly into a small cough. 'This Hunt Ball,' she asked, turning to look at him. 'What times does it start?'

'Oh, we'll drive over reasonably early,' he told her. 'Have to, as I'm on the committee. Got to greet everyone. That sort of thing. Did you get anything to wear?'

'No, Lucas,' she teased. 'I thought I'd come along in my silk nightie again, all right?'

He grinned. 'Fine by me.'

He swallowed his drink with unaccustomed haste. 'Look, I don't feel like going to Rosie's, but what about a bite to eat with old Martin? I warned him we might descend on him.'

'If you're sure . . .' she began doubtfully.

'Sure I'm sure, as they say in the movies.' He looked uncertain, though, and added, 'There's no knowing what sort of mood he's going to be in, so if he gets too unbearable we'll just walk out.' Goldie hoped it wouldn't come to that.

While she had a shower Lucas prowled about downstairs. She heard him put a tape of Vivaldi on, and take it off in favour of Bruce Springsteen. By the time she came out of the shower it was Nina Simone singing about love.

It didn't take her long to slip into the pink dress and put some make-up on. She only needed a little eye-liner and mascara, and a slick of lip-gloss to accentuate her tan. The pink dress brought out the subtle gold of her skin, and she surveyed the final effect in the mirror with satisfaction.

The dress, though demurely boned at the front, plunged dramatically at the back to a large bow that emphasised her tiny waist, and when she caught a glimpse of the back view in the mirror she wondered if perhaps it was a little too indiscreet for the sort of function she was about to attend. Never having been to a Hunt Ball before, she couldn't be sure.

'Lucas?' she called down. 'What do you think? Should I take a cover-up of some sort?'

He came slowly up the stairs, drink in hand. For a minute he stood on the landing without speaking. 'Looks all right to me,' he said at last.

Then she turned. 'That's what I mean,' she told him, looking over her shoulder at him. 'It plunges rather, and I thought maybe I should take a shawl of some sort. Or even the little velvet jacket?' she suggested.

She turned round again.

'Yes, take the jacket. It may be chilly,' he remarked, turning away abruptly.

Disappointed that he didn't seem to think much of her appearance, she went back into her room to fetch the jacket, then made her way downstairs to wait. She could hear him

splashing about in the shower, and there was a
drink already mixed for her on the table. Nina
Simone was still singing about love.

'Mr Martin's had a tiring day, sir. If you're
thinking of making your visit short, I'm sure
that will be best.' It was the housekeeper. She
showed them both in, and Lucas led the way
up a broad flight of stairs to a room on the
first floor. It was a dining-room, and Goldie
had a vague impression of a high ceiling hung
with a spectacular, unlit chandelier, and lots
of dark paintings in gold frames on the
rose-coloured walls, before her attention was
taken by a white-haired old man sitting in a
chair at the head of a long, polished table
reflecting the light of two large silver
candelabra.

''Bout time, Lucas. Never keep a man from
his dinner, or you'll get the worst of him.' He
peered across the room towards the door.
'Bring her in then, damn you. Let's have a
look at her.'

Lucas raised his eyebrows at Goldie, and
ushered her forward with one hand in the
small of her back. She stood demurely in front
of Martin de Maine, not quite sure what to
say, but taking his measure just as he was
taking hers.

'Spitting image of Ravella,' he judged,
peering from beneath shaggy brows. 'You've

got a handful there, me lad!' he cackled good-humouredly. 'Sit down, then, or are you both going to stand there all night? I hear it's this blessed ball come round again. You seem to spend half your time dancing these days.'

Lucas pulled out a chair for Goldie on the old man's right, and took the one opposite for himself. A servant came in with a trolley and Martin de Maine signalled towards the shadows. 'Get that bottle of claret I asked you to bring up,' he said to his man, and to Lucas he added, 'I've had me supper. Couldn't wait all night for you. But tuck in. Don't bother about me. I'm going to me room.' He patted Goldie on the hand. 'Tell Ravella "when lilacs last in the dooryard bloomed"—she'll know what I mean.' He gave a chuckle and, still smiling, was helped from the room by two of his staff.

'Typical!' Lucas gazed after him in disgust. 'Gets us up here, then disappears. I hope you're not offended?'

Goldie giggled. 'Honestly, I think I'm rather relieved, Lucas. He is rather formidable. I think he'd take a bit of getting used to.'

'You made a hit with him.'

'I did?' She laughed. 'How on earth can you tell?'

'I've known the old devil all my life.'

Goldie was relieved, although, as she was leaving in a few days, it didn't really matter. But she had thought he had left them because he didn't approve. It was a relief to learn otherwise.

'Now that's over,' said Lucas, swirling the claret round in his glass and looking thoughtful, 'I suppose——' He stopped.

Goldie leaned forward waiting for him to go on.

'Oh, nothing,' he said abruptly. He lifted the glass to his lips again. 'One thing,' he announced with the air of someone deftly changing the subject, 'he's got a fine cellar. Hope the old devil doesn't drink it all before I get a turn.' He laughed jerkily. 'You're not eating much.'

'You're beginning to sound like him,' she joked.

'Martin and I have nothing in common apart from our ancestry.'

And a penchant for my mother, thought Goldie silently, gnawing at the old jealousy.

It was just on nine as they made their way across the village green to one of the neighbouring houses where, as Lucas told her, the present master of foxhounds lived. Traditionally the annual ball was held in the master's house.

From this, Goldie assumed it was going to be a small affair, but she was mistaken. Not only was the long drive festooned with fairy lights—the whole house, though naturally much smaller than Burgh Hall, blazed with light, and on entering she discovered that there was a large ballroom at the back giving on to a terrace, and a lawn where a red and white marquee had been erected.

'Smoochy dancing in the ballroom,' Lucas informed her, 'disco stuff in the garden. We'll just stand by the door and say hello to a few people, then we're free to enjoy ourselves.'

Lucas's arrival had obviously been waited for. A red-faced man with iron-grey hair and a military bearing came up to him at once. 'Good to see you, Lucas, old chap. You can take over from me as doorman for a bit. I don't know who half these wallahs are. Never seen 'em out.' He slapped Lucas on the back, gave a nod of greeting to Goldie as if he felt he was expected to remember her, then unexpectedly said, 'Evening, Charlotte,' before disappearing in the direction of the drinks waiter before he could be corrected.

Goldie, vaguely wondering who Charlotte was and whether she would materialise at some stage, lost count of the people to whom she was introduced. Their politeness varied from effusive—Harold and some assorted cronies whom she recognised as the Saturday night crowd at the Coach and Horses—to the cool, in the shape of several dowdily dressed women she saw talking to Violet later, to the positively frigid—Rosemary, of course, who immediately took Lucas to task for not turning up for drinks first.

Lucas didn't give any explanation as to why he hadn't turned up, and Goldie knew that Rosemary put all the blame on her. She tried to ignore the unpleasant feeling she got, but it was difficult—especially when the name Charlotte cropped up again.

'She's looking absolutely ravishing tonight. But then, she always does. Such perfect taste! And so pretty with her lovely, traditional, English-rose looks.' Rosemary drifted off and her place was taken by another woman, small and plump where Rosemary was tall and rather gaunt.

'I'm looking for Charlotte, Lucas. You'll know where she is,' she began.

'I'm afraid I don't, Lucy. Why not try the marquee?' Lucas answered with a bland smile. Goldie smarted at the subtle arrows directed at her, and wondered if Lucas realised what was happening, but he smiled and remained polite, shook people's hands, and continued to introduce her to everyone. Later, when his stint as host was over, he led her firmly by the arm towards the buffet.

'I reckon we've earned this,' was all he said as he piled her plate with food. They found a place to sit down on some steps leading into a small ante-room jam-packed with people, and there was obviously little chance of finding a quiet corner. The whole place was bursting at the seams and new arrivals were coming in every minute.

'You mustn't let the guillotine mob get to you,' he observed casually, tucking into roast turkey. 'They don't mean to be bitchy. It's just that outsiders threaten all their matchmaking schemes.'

'And I suppose they have a scheme for you?' she observed tartly.

'As you've guessed.' He gave her a flash of white teeth. 'She's just making up her mind to come over and check you out.' He glanced across at a group of girls standing near one of the french windows, all looking their way. 'She's no doubt wondering why I'm ignoring her so thoroughly. I guess I'm going to have to have at least one dance with her. You won't mind?'

'Of course I'll damn well mind!' Goldie burst out with rather more vehemence than she'd intended. It was just at that moment that a tall pretty girl with soft brown curls and a self-confident manner came up to them, and, overhearing Goldie's outburst, turned to her with a little laugh. 'Goodness! You must be the American I've been hearing so much about. I gather Lucas has been showing you around a little bit?'

Her cornflower-blue eyes took in Goldie's flushed face at a glance, and before she could think of a reply the girl turned to Lucas. 'Darling Lukey, you shouldn't hide yourself away all evening. We're having such fun.' She put hand on his shoulder. 'Come and join us and don't be such a grouch.'

'Charlotte, I'm enjoying this rather fine roast turkey. Have you had yours?'

'Of course, but I don't mind sharing some of yours, too, darling. You know what a greedy girl I am!' She guided Lucas's fork to her own mouth. 'Mmm, scrumptious,' she murmured, slitting her eyes and looking at Lucas from beneath curling lashes.

Her lips are close enough to kiss Lucas's own, thought Goldie, feeling like a voyeur. And if she leans any closer, there's no way he'll be able to stop himself looking right down her cleavage. Lucas, to Goldie's chagrin, appeared to be enjoying Charlotte's rather too obvious attentions. He filled his fork again and popped it in her avaricious little Cupid's bow of a mouth.

'Now, go away, Charlotte,' he said firmly. 'I'll dance with you later.'

'I hope you mean it, Lucas. I missed you all

last week, having to go away to that wretched ski-school. I only got back this afternoon; that's why I haven't rung you. You're not cross with me, are you?' She obviously had no intention of going away, for she sat down on the step below Lucas and gazed up at him with large blue eyes.

Lucas was drawn into conversation, and Goldie felt that it was like the meeting in the hotel all over again, until she felt Lucas's knee against her own. Testing to see whether it was imagination or not, she moved her own away, but Lucas followed it, crushing right up against her as if by accident, and when she glanced hurriedly across at him he turned and gave her a sly wink.

'Come on, Goldie, let me dump your plate, then you can show me how they dance in California.' He pulled her to her feet. 'Excuse us, Charlotte. Your turn later.'

Goldie felt his hand in the small of her back. 'I thought the disco-dancing was in the marquee,' she said against the front of his shirt as he led her into a slow smooch.

'We'll try that later. Right now I think we need to get really close to each other.' He brushed her forehead with his lips and looked down at her, his eyes crinkling in amusement. 'I thought you were going to scratch her eyes out—or she yours,' he added fairly. 'I can't see what all the fuss is about. I do my own choosing.'

'Who are you choosing, Lucas?' she dared to ask.

'Who does it look like?'

Yes, she thought, comforted by his words, though not too much. But when I leave, who then?

CHAPTER NINE

IT WAS nearly time to go home. The evening had been more enjoyable than Goldie had expected, because even though she had had to witness Charlotte doing her best to wrap her body round Lucas's on the dance-floor—looking more like a rambling rose than an English rose, she thought with forgivable bitchiness—the crowd she called the Coach and Horses gang had amply made up for Lucas's tour of duty elsewhere, taking her under their wing and making sure she was never short of partners.

Flushed and happy, she went to the cloakroom to fetch her velvet jacket, but was stopped outside by a girl she recognised as one of Charlotte's friends. 'You know, you may think you can come between Charlotte and Lucas,' she said spitefully, barring the way, 'but you haven't really got a chance. He's annoyed with her tonight because she's been away. But he'll be ringing her up tomorrow as usual. You wait and see.'

'I'm sure that if he wishes to ring her up, he will,' replied Goldie as calmly as she could. She pushed her way past and went into the cloakroom. Inside, it was worse. Violet and Rosemary were deep in conversation, combing their hair and powdering their noses in the mirror as they talked. They didn't at first see Goldie.

'Burgh Hall, of course, needs a woman who's used to running a large staff,' Violet was saying conversationally. 'That will have to be his first priority, and I'm sure Martin has already warned him of the pitfalls of not having a suitable woman by his side.'

'Poor Martin,' sighed Rosemary. 'He always was one for the women—women of a certain type, that is.' She gave a little laugh. 'He regrets it now, of course, with only paid staff to look after him.' She turned to Violet. 'Charlotte is absolutely splendid for Lucas. She's used to his style. She can run Burgh Hall with one arm tied behind her back. It's obvious to everyone except Lucas himself. But, of course, he'll come round. Naturally, he's fighting like tooth and nail at the moment. They all do when the altar first looms on the horizon. Such a pity he has no one close to advise him. Still, Martin knows what's what. He's not likely to let Burgh Hall fall into the wrong hands.'

Goldie had been standing transfixed in the shadows by the door, unable to help hearing what they said, and too confused to move.

Now she forced herself to act, passing behind the two women so that her blonde hair was reflected in the mirror between them. She saw them exchange glances. To their credit, they fell silent until she had retrieved her jacket and was on her way out, but as she closed the door carefully behind her she heard Violet say, 'And that's exactly what I mean by the wrong hands.'

Goldie felt faint. She hadn't any designs on Lucas or Burgh Hall. But this evening had been so heavenly, they had seemed so close, so right for each other, she had begun to hope that it all meant something to him, after all. Now she saw the folly of her dreams. The two women were quite right—Lucas's inheritance was a responsibility. He would need help. The sort of help she could never imagine herself being able to give.

With a heavy heart she made her way back to where he was waiting in the hall. As usual, he was surrounded by a group of old friends. They were laughing about something that had happened to a mutual acquaintance, and Goldie waited patiently with a weeping heart and a fixed smile as Lucas said his goodbyes.

'All right, lovely?' he asked, eyes dancing as they made their way outside. He hugged her as the cold night air hit them. 'You look a little sad,' he murmured. 'Are you tired?'

She nodded, unable to confess the burden in her heart.

When they reached the millhouse he hesitated in the entrance, his white silk scarf a blur in the darkness. 'Goldie,' he said, his voice husky with desire, 'there's only one real way to finish this evening. Tell me before we go inside. It's got to be your decision. Only know I want you, desperately and forever.'

She felt her body quiver from head to foot. He didn't touch her, but she could feel his eyes on her face in the darkness. In two days she would leave this man, for good and all. It was a thought too agonising to face. Surely, she prayed, they deserved some happiness together? She wanted him, and she longed to have him remember this night to the end of his days.

Standing on tiptoe, she reached up in the darkness and placed her lips on his. With a sudden wild joy she felt him take her powerfully into his arms.

'My love!' The words were wrenched from his throat, and, with a surge of happiness that only destiny could have had a hand in, she felt him gather her slim body against his own and, with a fever of longing lending him haste, take her at last into the house—into her house of dreams.

The night passed in a delirium of ecstasy.

Goldie had never been loved by a man before, and Lucas carried her to the summits of a passion she had only guessed at. Playing her body with all the skills only a man in love could command, he made her an instrument of pure pleasure. She gave herself to him entirely, submitting to the heaven of his touch with no thought of the pain of separation to come.

When day broke she was lying in the crook of his arm, her head resting lightly on his chest. His hand idled through the platinum strands of her cropped hair, the other caressed her silky gold skin as if it belonged to him, and to him alone. 'I love you, Goldie. We were destined for each other from the start,' he told her, pulling her on top of him. 'I love your eyes, your hair, your skin, your smile, your sadness, even.' He stroked her cheek. 'You are sad, aren't you? Can't I make you happy?' His eyes darkened with pain as he saw that what he said was true. She didn't have that look of happiness that a woman who has been truly loved should have. Instead of answering, she rolled away, burying her face in the pillow beside his head. His lips came down on the nape of her neck.

'What do I have to do to make you happy, darling? Tell me, I'll do anything. Anything at all. Just ask.'

'It's not that, Lucas,' she mumbled into the pillow. 'It's not you. It's just life. I didn't know love was like this. Making love.'

'Did I hurt you?'

'Of course not.' How could she explain that his touch brought only joy and ecstasy, and that was why she felt such anguish now—knowing that it would be something soon to be denied her forever?

He held her in his arms until the sun was up. 'Listen,' he told her, shaking her awake as she lay drowsily, half dreaming that their parting was only an insubstantial nightmare, 'I have to get up. You can stay here if you like. Or come with me.'

'I don't want to stay without you.' She blinked open her eyes. 'Where are you going to?'

'I've got to go to church, OK? You'll come with me?'

She nodded.

Soon they were ready to go. Lucas was transformed into a pillar of respectability in a dark suit and crisp white shirt, his black hair groomed into order. Goldie wore a grey velvet coat—something she had bought with him in mind. On her head was a small pink hat, coquettishly smart.

'You look ravishing.' He pulled her into his arms and kissed her slow and long on the lips, already his fingers at the buttons of her blouse.

'Are we going or staying?' she asked, submitting instantly to the urgency of his need as it transmitted itself to every cell in her body. She was disappointed when he scowled at the clock.

'I have to be there, so let me go, you witch. We'll come back the instant it's over.'

Unsure of the propriety of such a remark, with a dreamy smile, she allowed him to fasten her buttons. The day would last forever in her memory. It would be hers for life. All she asked was that they spent every minute together.

When they reached the tiny church at the other end of the village, the bell was already concluding its final Sunday morning summons. Through the great oak door she could see all the pews full of people. 'There doesn't seem to be room,' she remarked. 'Do we stand at the back?'

Without replying he tucked her hand firmly in his and set off down the centre aisle, footsteps echoing hollowly so that heads turned to watch. Self-conscious at the entrance they were making, Goldie raised her head proudly, trusting Lucas to know what to do. He led them past the full rows, the curious glances, past the brass lectern in the shape of a golden eagle, down to the very front until, unfastening a wooden gate in a row of empty pews facing the small choir, he ushered her in. Here there was space, and suddenly she knew why. 'De Maine' it said in ancient script over the back of the wooden stalls. And there was an image of the heraldic animal she was beginning to understand was the sign of the de Maine family.

All eyes were on them still. She tilted her head. Rosemary Lancaster was sitting on the front row adjacent to them, first in the row of unmarked pews. Her lips tightened in disapproval at the sight of Lucas and his mistress sitting so brazenly in the sight of God. Recognising this, Goldie raised her head proudly. If what she had done was wrong, then so be it. There was surely mercy enough in the world to forgive her the sin of loving Lucas de Maine? She slipped her hand into his as the congregation rose.

Not much later she understood his haste to be here, for he squeezed her hand once before letting it go. Then, rising to his feet, he made his way in the echoing silence to the lectern—handsome, erect and proud—and, in a deep voice of penetrating power, began to read the lesson.

Goldie felt that there was nothing so beautiful in the world as Lucas de Maine reading aloud in the hushed stillness of the ancient church. The syllables rolled around the stone vault with all the authority of the ancient line from which he descended. It made her sacrifice have meaning, for there was no way she could hope to join her wayward blood with his.

They were expected to leave first, after the vicar led the way, standing in the porch as if to advertise their love. If anyone had had any doubts about her presence by his side, Lucas's intentions were made clear by the looks he gave her. She felt naked under his sparkling gaze, proud to be so, though she heard the word 'brazen' and saw the whispers behind raised hands when Lucas wasn't looking.

They returned to the millhouse as soon as they could. He had stripped her before she reached the foot of the stairs. She felt his hardness penetrate the yielding core of her being, crying out in the joy of submitting to the demands of his male pride.

'Do you love me, Goldie?' he demanded as he possessed her body again and again. 'Say the words to me, darling, let me hear you say it aloud.' So far she had been unable to admit to what was closest to her, fearing it would bind her to him somehow, and her sacrifice would become impossible.

Even now, demand and cajole and curse as he did, she could not allow herself to say the words. She knew it was driving him to despair, that to possess her body was only half his desire, but her lips were sealed.

He asked her again in the stillness of the night. He asked her as dawn broke and, hours later, as she said goodbye at the airport, he asked her once again.

'I can't say what I know wouldn't be right to say,' she told him, turning her head. Her heart was breaking, but the life that would soon close round him, claiming him for the bride who waited for him, haunted her mind.

They were parted soon by officialdom. His face looked grey, standing out in a sea of strangers, diminishing, soon impossible to discern. Then she was airborne; the airport, soon England itself, diminished and faded from view.

CHAPTER TEN

GOLDIE returned home and took up life much where she had left it. The four months in the mountains turned out to be only two, as a part came her way that she felt was just right, and after she'd worked on that she felt drained and retreated to the mountains again. Ravella saw the rushes and rang her straight away.

'I didn't know you had it in you, darling. I'd got you down as a light-comedy actress. You have real dramatic power. I'm so proud.'

'Don't get too pleased about it. I'm thinking of giving it up for good.'

'Darling, I think I'm coming to see you.'

'I thought you were in the middle of a film?'

'So what?'

Two days later Ravella came walking up the stony path that led to Goldie's cabin, wearing peacock-blue beach trousers, a matching shirt over a bra top, and lots of gold chains. Goldie, lying on the sun-deck in a scrap of a bikini, heard her before she saw her, and raised herself on to one elbow, but didn't get up.

'You're looking beautifully golden, but aren't you rather thin?' Ravella sank down into one of the loungers, depositing a pile of presents at her feet. 'That's quite a walk up from the village. I must be older than I look.'

'You've always been older than you look.' Goldie lay back and closed her eyes.

'I suppose it's a man,' Ravella began. 'I would think I'm just about the best person to turn to for advice on that topic.'

Goldie smiled grudgingly. 'I expect you are.'

Ravella got up and went into the house, and came back with two gin fizzes. 'I can't imagine who he is. Not a breath of rumour has come my way.' She frowned. 'I wonder if I'm getting out of touch?'

'I doubt it. There's no way you could have heard about us.'

'Ah . . .' Ravella sipped her drink. 'Not one of the film crowd, then?'

'Emphatically not.'

'I suppose,' said Ravella carefully, 'that means England . . . I heard you'd been over there just after Eva died.'

'Oh, shut up, Mother! I don't want to talk about him. I knew it was impossible from the minute I set eyes on him. I'll get over him in time.'

'I really don't see why you should have to if you really want him. What's the point of that?'

Goldie didn't answer.

'You're not trying to tell me this mystery man is unattracted to you?'

'For goodness' sake!' She scowled. 'That doesn't really come into it.'

'Ah . . .'

'And will you stop saying "ah" every few minutes, like some third-rate detective?'

'Listen to me, child.' Ravella smiled, knowing she was playing up to her role as mother, but genuinely concerned by the unhappiness she saw in Goldie's face. 'The best advice I can give you is go back to him. If he reacts favourably, tell him you care.'

'He must know how I feel,' she mumbled, 'but feelings can't alter facts.'

Ravella looked out over the valley that fell away beyond the terrace. It was so beautiful, it hurt the eyes. But Goldie seemed oblivious to her surroundings.

'Does that mean he's married?'

'Of course not, for heaven's sake!'

Ravella seemed to give a sigh of relief. 'Then I can't see how the problem can be serious.' When Goldie didn't reply, she went on, 'Darling, I'm here to help. I do know what you're going through, really I do.'

'You? That's rich! What do you know about *real* love?' A memory of something

Lucas had said when they had first met came back to taunt her. She sat up, glaring across at her mother with all her misery showing in her eyes.

'That could be hurtful, Goldie,' replied Ravella softly, 'if I thought you knew the truth.'

'What truth?'

A faraway look came into her mother's eyes. 'It's true I have flitted from man to man until recently, and I suppose I haven't been a good example of fidelity for you. But one thing I can put my hand on my heart and say—if your father hadn't been killed in that car crash before you were born, I would have been the most loving, faithful, one-man wife ever.' She paused and her voice thickened. 'When he died, my life seemed to end.'

Goldie picked up the sun-tan oil and started to dot it over her legs. 'You hardly ever talked about him when I was little. I grew up knowing next to nothing about him.'

'I'm sorry, darling, it was simply too painful to mention his name. He was the *best*,' she said quietly. 'That was my own personal nightmare, and I fought my way through it. I *had* to, I had to bring you up. You were the most precious thing in the world to me—a part of him I would always have.' She picked up a pair of dark glasses and slipped them on. 'I was lucky in that I had Eva and Brendan.

Together they helped me pull through.'

'Brendan?' Goldie looked up. 'Yes, I heard something about Brendan from——' She stopped abruptly, unable to say his name in the detached tone the conversation warranted.

Ravella gave her a swift glance. 'When Eva rejected Brendan, he turned to me,' she said. 'We were lovers, then good friends—at least, that's all it seemed. I realised when it was too late that for Brendan it had meant much more. That last summer must have been hell for him. The de Maine men are really quite something, and by then I'd known them all such a long, long time, it was natural to share myself between them.' She went on, 'You won't remember Willett, though I expect you met Martin when you were over there?' It was a question tacked on so skilfully that Goldie nodded before she could think.

'And Willett's son?' asked Ravella gently.

Goldie turned away. 'Did you have affairs with all three of them, then?' she demanded in a tight voice.

Ravella laughed. 'Willett was married and adultery isn't my style, though I knew he would always be there for me if the time was right. But, yes, after the thing with Brendan seemed to fizzle out, I had a brief fling with Martin. He'd always played the disapproving older brother, and it was fun to get him to thaw. It was quite a revelation to discover what a wicked devil he was on the quiet. He was the type who never had any intention of marrying. He never did marry, and he never wanted to. Some men are like that. Some women, too, because Eva was the same. The two of them should have split their differences and lived together, but of course in those days that wasn't done. Oh,' she stretched her arms to the sky, 'what a tangled web we weave.'

'There's a message from Martin for you,' remembered Goldie with a start of guilt. 'I forgot about it till now. Something about lilacs and dooryards.'

'Whitman.' Ravella quoted the line and the rest of the poem in her husky actress's voice. 'The darling,' she said softly. 'I hope I'll be able to go over soon. It's good to go back into the past sometimes. It helps to root out old ideas that have gone wrong.'

She leaned forward, removing the sunglasses, but Goldie could still see the moisture on the dark lashes. 'What was his name?' she asked. 'I'm not sure I can remember.' Goldie saw her frown, the clear green eyes on her own.

'Whose name?' she asked, dropping her glance.

'Willett's son's name, of course.'

Goldie picked up the sun-tan oil and screwed the cap on more firmly before mumbling, 'Lucas, actually.'

'Ah, yes, Lucas.' Ravella fell silent.

'Well, what about it?' asked Goldie truculently.

Ravella puckered her brow. 'Isn't he rather young for you? He's surely only about fifteen.'

'Mother, time has passed since you were there, and not everybody keeps on having the same birthday like you.'

Ravella ignored this and said, 'So he's now around twenty-six or twenty-seven?'

'Twenty-seven next month.' Goldie wished she could have bitten off her tongue. Why else would she remember some man's birthday unless she had a more than passing interest? It was no use now. She gave her mother a look of resignation. 'You may as well have it. I just happen to love him,' she mumbled. 'I can't help it. It's horrible. I want to die.'

Ravella came to sit on the edge of the sun-bed, taking Goldie in her arms and holding her as if she were a little girl.

'I went back for the auction,' she mumbled into her mother's peacock-blue blouse. 'I thought I might be able to rescue that painting of us. Do you remember it? But Lucas bought it for some mysterious client, and—well, that's how we met.'

'If he's anything like his father, he'll be a handsome devil. But the faithful type. A good man. Rare these days. Goldie, what can I say?

There's only one thing to tell you. Go back. Risk it.'

'It's no good, he's got to marry some girl who'll look after Burgh Hall.'

'They can afford a housekeeper, surely?'

'Of course. But everybody says he needs somebody who'll look the part. An English rose.'

Ravella laughed. 'Is that all that's stopping you?' She stroked Goldie's hair back from her face. It had grown quickly, and now almost reached her shoulders. 'You're an actress, aren't you?' she whispered. 'Put it to good use,' and before Goldie could protest she went on, 'And, anyway, it's type-casting—look at this place. You love it up here. You're in your element in the countryside.'

'I know. But Lucas doesn't know that.'

'Then go back and tell him. Go back, Goldie. Look beautiful for him. And if he's half the man the rest of the de Maines were, you won't have to do a thing.'

Goldie was more than half persuaded, but she couldn't help saying, 'If he really wanted me, he'd have come after me.'

'Nonsense. He probably thinks you have half the film moguls in Hollywood at your feet. And, anyway, he's a farmer first. Had you forgotten? What time of year is it over there?'

'Mid-summer, I expect.'

'There you are, then. One of the busiest times of the year. He can't just walk out on it all. Crops won't stop growing just because Lucas de Maine wants a rest.'

'I'd forgotten about all that.'

'You'll have to start remembering.'

Goldie felt more cheerful than she had for months. 'It'll be better to *do* something, instead of sitting up here wishing,' she told her mother. She kissed her on the forehead. 'Thanks, Mum.'

When she arrived at Heathrow she was feeling less sure of herself than when she'd been sitting on the sun-deck of her mountain cabin. It was easy to be swept along on the tide of Ravella's enthusiasm, she realised, as she made her way through Customs. But what if Lucas had married in the time that had elapsed? What if he really had seen her as just another sex-obsessed starlet? And what if that grey, haggard look on his face as he had said goodbye was simply the effect of a couple of sleepless nights?

Oh, let him love me, God, she prayed as the taxi carried her across London to the railway station.

She hadn't stopped to work out a plan of campaign, and when she eventually alighted at York station where a hire car was waiting she still didn't know how she was going to approach him. Should she ring first and ask to see him? Or would it be best to turn up on his doorstep? Either way, she could see it might lead to awkwardness, for there would be no way she could make it look like a casual call.

Still undecided when she reached the village soon after lunch, she drove slowly down the main street, hoping against hope that he would suddenly emerge in her path and her worst fears would be quickly allayed. But the street was empty, the only signs of life a few ducks emerging from the pond on the green.

As she had told Ravella, it was mid-summer in England. The trees she remembered for their spare angularity were now swathed in the full beauty of high summer, and the fields shone with the brilliance of new life, pregnant with their annual bounty and softly bound by hedgerows made hazy with sweet umbrils of Old Man's Beard. Its beauty made her ache with a renewed sense of time passing, taking all with it.

Deciding her safest approach would be to call on Hetty Woollard first, she reasoned that Hetty would be sure to let her know at once whether her journey had been wasted or not. At the same time she could hand over the little present she had brought with her for the new baby.

Carefully she accelerated up the lane made narrow by rampantly flowering verges, turning into the drive opposite the millhouse without daring to cast her glance in that direction. She pulled up and switched off the engine.

In the deep silence of the countryside, rooks set up a sudden clamour in the elms, and from a distant farmyard a dog began to bark.

Suddenly another nearer sound caught her attention. Climbing out of the car, she crossed the drive to the house. A pram stood outside the front porch and she bent to look inside. Hetty's grandchild gurgled happily within. Goldie felt something tug deep at the core of her being as she watched the tiny hands flail at the gaily coloured baubles strung from the hood.

'Goldie! Bless my soul!' It was Hetty standing in the doorway, a bunch of cut flowers from the garden in her arms.

'Isn't she adorable?' Goldie sighed still bending over the pram.

'I've got her to myself today.' Hetty looked pleased. 'You couldn't have come at a better time. But what a surprise, you should have warned us!' She gave her a quick hug. 'Mother all right?'

'Fine.' Goldie looked back at the pink and white bundle in the pram. 'I didn't realise they were so tiny.'

'Nearly six months now,' Hetty told her

proudly. 'Would you like to hold her?' She extracted the kicking infant from the pram, and together they went over to the wooden seat on the front lawn. Goldie took the baby gingerly in her arms.

'She's beautiful,' she breathed, gazing down at the soft bundle.

Just then there was the sound of footsteps on the gravel, and as she looked up she heard them come to an abrupt halt. Then her blood froze. Only yards away, Lucas himself was staring down at her, a look of horrified amazement on his features. He moved forward with two or three dogs arching at his feet, then came to a sudden halt again.

'Come to admire my granddaughter, Lucas?' called Hetty, looking up.

'Yours?' He seemed to pull himself together. Bringing a smile to his lips, he came towards the two women, but when he got close enough Goldie could see that his eyes, unlike his lips, were unsmiling. They swept over her, touching her face, her hair, her slim form, with calculated indifference. She was glad she was wearing what she wanted to wear, and not some concoction designed to please the farmer in him, as Ravella had suggested. Her tan cotton dress was sleeveless, and her wheat-coloured hair just brushed its white lace collar. She felt cool and sophisticated and in control. She crossed her feet in their tiny white court shoes, and hugged the baby to her.

'When did you arrive?' he asked coolly.

'A few minutes ago,' she admitted.

'On holiday again?'

She nodded.

'Life's one long holiday for some,' he observed.

'You'll stay for a cup of tea, Lucas?' Hetty was already on her feet, and Goldie suspected it was tact that made her disappear so swiftly indoors.

'How long are you staying?' he asked when she'd gone.

'It depends,' she replied carefully. All her plans seemed to be in ruins now he had turned up before she could work out the lie of the land from Hetty.

'Depends on what turns up for you, I suppose,' his lip curled, 'in your usual *laissez-faire* style.' He still stood on the path, hands in pockets, looking down at her from a distance.

Taking her courage in both hands, she said, 'It depends on you, really, Lucas. I came to see you.'

'From California?'

She stroked the top of the baby's head, a knot of anguish rising so rapidly into her throat, she found it impossible to answer. He was still standing on the gravel, as if to come near her was something to be avoided.

She felt her limbs begin to tremble. In a

minute he would tell her he was married, or
engaged, or simply wish her good day and
walk off back into his own life without
another glance. Her stricken eyes lifted to his,
and for a moment she met his dark ones in a
silent exchange, as if time had started to go
backwards.

'I thought the baby was yours,' he said
abruptly, pushing one of the dogs down as it
jumped up at him and tried to lick his face.

She gave a wry smile. 'Hardly,' she
remarked, tearing her glance away and
pretending to straighten the baby's pink
blanket.

'I'll just see to these dogs, then I'll be back.'
He whistled twice and the dogs loped after him
round the side of the house.

He returned a few seconds later. 'I've told
Hetty I haven't time for tea. I'm busy right
now. Come over and see me if you feel like it.'
He gave her a curt nod and she watched him
walk away with just his own gun dog at his
heels, until he reached the gate and turned off
behind the trees.

When Hetty returned with a tray she helped
Goldie put the baby back in its pram, then sat
down beside her on the seat. As Hetty poured
the tea from its silver pot, Goldie took a deep
breath and remarked as casually as she could,
'There was talk of Lucas and Charlotte being
together last time I was here . . .'

'Still is. Talk, that is. You know what small villages are like,' Hetty smiled pleasantly.

'So they're not engaged or anything?' She had to know.

Hetty gave a light laugh. 'Lucas isn't the hapless victim these women like to think . . . He's a de Maine through and through,' she added, as if that explained everything.

Goldie didn't know whether to laugh or cry. 'It was a shock seeing him,' she muttered.

'Shock or no, you get yourself over there as soon as you've had a nice cup of tea.' Hetty patted her on the arm. 'You're looking lovely, Goldie. Your mother must be really proud of you.'

Fortified by Hetty's words, Goldie delayed as long as she dared, then, plucking up courage, walked over the road to the millhouse. Lucas was in the garden, sitting at a wooden table, a pile of ledgers spread out in front of him and a bottle of rosé and two glasses, one of them half-empty, on the table as well. He poured her a glass without speaking, refilled his own, raised it, then drank as if in a silent toast.

'Well?' he said carefully, replacing the glass beside him and taking up his pen as if he was about to continue work.

'Make it easy for me, Lucas.' She stood uncertainly beside the table, as he hadn't invited her to sit down, trailing the ribbons of her straw sun-hat over and over between her fingers.

'Easy?' He looked at her as if he didn't know what she meant.

She stood unhappily in front of him while he fiddled with his pen, glancing down at the ledger as if he'd rather she left right away, and she had chance to note how much thinner he seemed, his hair longer, his eyes more hooded, the cheekbones more pronounced, and the hollows beneath them correspondingly darker. He was wearing the old fawn sweater with the patches on the elbows, and a pair of quite decent jeans, with black jodhpur boots, as if he'd just been riding or was just about to go out. Already the summer sun had burned his face to a deep, even bronze.

Abruptly he flung down his pen and got up. 'This is damned useless!' He didn't say what, but moved round the side of the table towards her and stood looking down at her with a hard mouth.

'I don't make the same mistake twice over. It's not my way.' Then, before she could say anything, he started to stroll off down the garden. She decided she'd better follow, and when they reached the gate at the bottom she saw him lean on it, looking out across a buttercup-filled meadow to the hills beyond.

'I was thinking about Ravella the other day,' he told her after a long pause. 'She was treated so badly by the gossipmongers—not because of anything she did while she was here, breaking the odd heart or two,' he smiled bitterly, 'but for the grave sin of actually daring to leave. It was regarded as a judgement on them. And people don't like that.'

Before Goldie could say anything, he went on, 'There's something to be said for having no roots. At least you're free.' He gave a twisted smile. 'You're the ones that got away.' He looked away again, and Goldie followed his glance across the meadow to the copse and further to the blue haze of the summer hills beyond.

'It can't be any burden to you being heir to all this, Lucas.' She turned her head to where she could see the rolling parkland of the estate, with its line of ancient beeches marking the drive to Burgh Hall. This was her own idea of paradise. If it were hers she would never dream of leaving.

'We're fastened in here as tight as cattle in a pen,' he said bitterly. 'I've done my share of globe-trotting, and maybe that's my problem—I can't settle anywhere now. But I have to, don't I? I have a duty. Every time I see that damned family tree in the church I know I'm rooted in for life.' He smiled ironically. 'The burden of kingship.'

He turned to look down at her. 'I guess I should count my blessings. But when it means losing the one person I know I could be happy with—well, what should I feel?'

'Lucas?' Goldie couldn't bear to see him look like this. She felt an overwhelming desire to take his dark head between her hands and kiss all the sorrow away, but she was held back by the fear that he was telling her all this for some other reason, and could only say, 'It's not so brilliant having no roots, you know. Belonging nowhere. Being an outcast for life. My mother thrives on it. I'm different, I like to belong. I like a simple life.'

'You?' He turned, something stirring deep in the dark eyes.

'I've spent most of the last six months, since——' she bit her lip '—since leaving, living by myself in the mountains. I told you I was going to do it. I wanted to find out what I really wanted.'

'And did you?' he cut in sharply.

She nodded. 'I think so. It was obvious, really. But it took a lot of soul-searching to pluck up the courage to come back and put my head on the block.' She tried to laugh, but it came out like a sob, and then suddenly Lucas had his arms around her and she felt their two bodies seek and find each other. Then his lips, the lips she had longed for, came down sweetly to cover her own, trembling with long-pent desire.

'Oh, Lucas, I hated leaving you. But we

seemed like total opposites. I dared not admit I loved you. They all said you needed someone like Charlotte. And you asked me in that horrible tone of voice whether I could see myself running Burgh Hall, and I couldn't, and—oh, it all seemed so hopeless. I thought the only loving thing I could do was leave and let you get on with your life as it was meant to be, but, Lucas, I've been so unhappy without you. Can it work? Do you care? Please, Lucas, tell me, even if it's to say no. Put me out of my misery, please, Lucas—oh, Lucas . . .' Her voice changed as his body told her in a way more eloquent than words that all her fears were fantasy.

'I loved and wanted you from the minute I saw you in that auction-room with your clothes falling off all the time. I knew you were the little butterfly I needed to make this place bearable. To hell with what the village think. Only *I* know what I need. And it's you, Goldie. Always and only you.'

He rocked her back and forth in his arms, plying her with sweet kisses till she felt she would faint with rapture.

'Goldie, I prayed you would become a moth instead of a butterfly. Someone who preferred muddy country lanes to city streets, the simple life to the glamorous life, Land Rovers,' he smiled, 'to fast sports cars, and wellington boots instead of high-heeled silver ones. And then I thought, if you were like that I wouldn't love you half as much.'

'But, Lucas,' she murmured as he slid his hand down the back of her dress, 'I like all of those things and more. But, most important of all, I like you. And whatever you're doing and wherever you are, I want to be there beside you.' She looked up at him from beneath long lashes and asked, 'Don't male butterflies live in the country, too? I mean ones that wear a kind of country camouflage that makes them look like moths, when at heart they're really butterflies in disguise?'

'Do you know anything about the countryside, my darling?'

'Probably more than you realise, dear Lucas. But I'm willing to learn whatever you want to teach me.'

'Then, Goldie, let me teach you first what it's like to make love in an English meadow full of flowers.' With masterful ease he lifted her over the gate, and as she leaned against him he slithered the cotton dress over her head before she could protest. Pulling her golden body down into the long grass, he then began to love her as she had always dreamed he would, and, her senses swooning under the lyrical onslaught of his touch, she became his creature of the hills and dales, his butterfly of the wild wood.

*   *   *

Later he told her what she would have to expect as his wife. 'A white wedding in the village church. An infant or two as soon as possible. Church fêtes and bazaars to be opened. The refurbishment of Burgh Hall——'

'You mean we'll be living there?'

'Martin insists. In fact, he told me so the day after he met you. ''Don't let her get away like Ravella did.'' But I couldn't come after you to tell you, because I thought it was the last thing you wanted.'

'I don't object to Burgh Hall as long as you're in it.'

'There's another thing.' He frowned. 'I don't like country wives with nothing on their minds but gossip and the making of jam. You'll have to keep up this career of yours. And, besides, I like the idea of a famous wife.'

'I've been thinking about that,' she told him seriously, 'I'd like to make just one good film a year. I don't need to do the rubbish because we don't need the money. And I've got to the stage where I'm able to pick and choose. It'll fit in with children, too. I'm not going off without them all the time.'

'Where you go, they go, and where they go, I go——'

'And vice versa,' she said, not caring if it didn't make strict sense.

He kissed her. 'That's settled, then. Next

time we get dressed, we'd better show our faces in the village. The sooner everybody has chance to get used to you, the better.'

Later he took her up to be presented formally to Martin de Maine. The engagement ring was, he apologised, a tradition for de Maine brides. Martin would hand it over to her himself.

One of the first things she noticed when she entered the sitting-room at Burgh Hall was a painting over the mantelpiece. It was of a woman in blue with long fair hair and a baby on her lap. 'Your client was Martin?' she asked in surprise.

'The sentimental old fool. He gave me orders to buy it at any price. It must mean he's got some sort of heart underneath that hard-as-nails exterior. I think he was secretly in love with Ravella from the very beginning.'

Just then Martin himself came in, looking fitter than ever and obviously feeling on top of the world. 'You may as well move in now, because I intend to be around to see the next generation on its way, and you don't want to be bringing up de Maines in a hovel.' He looked accusingly at Lucas. 'She's a real beauty, but what's the matter with *you*? Nearly lost her, didn't you?' He patted Goldie on the shoulder. 'If he ever lets you down, come to me. I'll sort the young devil out for you.' Part of the sorting out was to give Lucas a proper income from the estate.

Later, Lucas took Goldie in his arms, a frown on his face. 'It's true. I very nearly did lose you,' he reproached himself. 'I intended to propose after Martin gave his tacit approval that first evening you met him, but I wasn't sure you'd say yes just then. It would have looked as if I was rushing you. But I wish to heaven I'd risked it. We might have saved ourselves the hell of the last six months.'

'It doesn't matter now, Lucas, the past is finished with. We have the future to look forward to.'

'The past is never finished,' he corrected, 'but the future belongs to us, and the present, too.' With a sigh of pleasure she felt his lips take her own, and she knew she was home at last.

A Mother's Day Treat

This beautifully packaged set of 4 brand new Romances makes an ideal choice of Mother's Day gift.

BLUEBIRDS IN THE SPRING
Jeanne Allen
THE ONLY MAN
Rosemary Hammond
MUTUAL ATTRACTION
Margaret Mayo
RUNAWAY
Kate Walker

These top authors have been selected for their blend of styles, and with romance the key ingredient to all the storylines, what better way to treat your mother... or even yourself.

Available from February 1990.
Price £5.40

From: Boots, Martins, John Menzies, W.H. Smith, Woolworths and other paperback stockists.

2 NEW TITLES FOR JANUARY 1990

Mariah by Sandra Canfield is the first novel in a sensational quartet of sisters in search of love… Mariah's sensual and provocative behaviour contrasts enigmatically with her innocent and naive appearance… Only the maverick preacher can recognise her true character and show her the way to independence and true love.

£2.99

Faye is determined to make a success of the farm she has inherited – but she hadn't accounted for the bitter battle with neighbour, Seth Carradine, who was after the land himself. In desperation she turns to him for help, and an interesting bargain is struck. **Kentucky Woman** by Casey Douglas, best-selling author of Season of Enchantment. **£2.99**

W●RLDWIDE

SOLITAIRE – Lisa Gregory £3.50

Emptiness and heartache lay behind the facade of Jennifer Taylor's glittering Hollywood career. Bitter betrayal had driven her to become a successful actress, but now at the top, where else could she go?

SWEET SUMMER HEAT – Katherine Burton £2.99

Rebecca Whitney has a great future ahead of her until a sultry encounter with a former lover leaves her devastated...

THE LIGHT FANTASTIC – Peggy Nicholson £2.99

In this debut novel, Peggy Nicholson focuses on her own profession... Award-winning author Tripp Wetherby's fear of flying could ruin the promotional tour for his latest blockbuster. Rennie Markell is employed to cure his phobia, whatever it takes!

These three new titles will be out in bookshops from February 1990.

W RLDWIDE

Available from Boots, Martins, John Menzies, W.H. Smith, Woolworths and other paperback stockists.